To
Valerie & R.
With Love.   15 March 18.
Bryan x

C000270726

SECRET DEMON
BOOK 2

C. L. Ryan x.

First Published in Great Britain 2017 by Mirador Publishing

Copyright © 2017 by C. L. Ryan

All rights reserved. No part of this publication may be reproduced or transmitted, in any form or by any means, without permission of the publishers or author. Excepting brief quotes used in reviews.

First edition: 2017

Any reference to real names and places are purely fictional and are constructs of the author. Any offence the references produce is unintentional and in no way reflects the reality of any locations or people involved.

A copy of this work is available through the British Library.

ISBN: 978-1-911473-72-5

Mirador Publishing
Mirador
Wearne Lane
Langport
Somerset
TA10 9HB

Secret Demon
Book 2

C. L. Ryan
www.angelicalskies.com

TABLE OF CONTENTS

THE BRIGHT YELLOW DOOR!

Watch out! Watch out!
There's a demon about.
He's nasty and evil, and will fill you with fear.
He'll make your life miserable unable to bear.
"Where is he?" asked the angel of the master above.
"Look to the darkness, the place that he loves."
"I spy the beggar," said the angel who stood looking
from afar.
"He's sat on the roof of a house over there!"
"Which one?" said the master, asking for more.
"It's the little one there with the bright yellow door!"
WHAT COLOUR IS YOUR DOOR?

Chapter 1

1969

It's 1969, and situation normal in the Murphy family house: absolute flippin' mayhem! As usual. Megan was recovering well; she was still shocked at the bullying she had endured over the last 3 years, and was still trying to take in the fact that she had actually tried to kill herself, but day by day she was making progress and gaining the strength and confidence needed to face the problematic life that lay ahead. Her third eye had now started to open, much to the delight of her angels, Sally, Claire and Elaine, who kept a constant vigil on her without Megan even knowing it.

Her demon still called to her trying to connect and continued to scratch outside her window at night. She was still hearing the baby crying, and every night she heard the footsteps going up and down the staircase. Unseen the angels stood guard in her bedroom, protecting her from the spirit people who were now popping in and out trying to communicate with Megan. Sometimes they would frighten her by talking unexpectedly, making her jumpy and very nervous at times, especially when this occurred in the middle of the night when the room was in darkness.

Patsy however, was starting to drink more; she was struggling with her demon, making her moody, with regular violent outbursts which always seemed to be focused on Megan, Trixie and their father Tom.

Patsy was working at a local jam factory and at times seemed to struggle with her work and home life. Her main focus was always on her husband Tom, and she was constantly asking herself where he was and who he was talking to. She was trying hard not to listen to the demon who was forever talking in her head, trying to stir up trouble. It was hard, really hard, and sometimes she was too weak, and he took over, making her violent, and lash out at the nearest person to her, which always seemed to be either Megan or her little sister Trixie. So life for her was becoming a slog, an unbearable slog. She never laughed, sang or seemed to be happy any more, and without realising it, had become ever more dependent on Megan to help her support the family.

Tom on the other hand was struggling with his home life completely. Money was short, and whilst his job at the marble company was reliable it was not very well paid, and with 2 families to support, one there and the other in Gory, Southern Ireland, the pressure to work away was mounting. When he was at home, Patsy could be difficult to live with, moody and aggressive. Consequently he spent most of his time down the allotments or in the pigeon loft preparing his birds for the next long race, when the new season started, and after one particular month of Patsy ranting and raving, and watching her being totally unpleasant to both Megan and Trixie, but never the two boys, he decided that he'd had enough. He often questioned why he had ever agreed to let himself be in that situation, and the burden of the secret weighed heavy upon him. He felt that Patsy was changing, and he didn't like what he saw unravelling in front of his eyes. Sometimes he feared for the safety of his children, the two girls especially, but he also felt alone, and had no one to speak to. Father Thomas Jones had gone back to Oxford University to study Demonology to try and help him, but he had heard nothing from him for months, and his heart weighed heavy.

He loved his beautiful wife, and prayed every day thanking the Lord above for the gift of his wonderful children who he could never be without, but he was finding that living in that house was oppressive and strange. Neighbours and relatives never liked visiting, and when they did they never stayed very long, all seeming to sense the extra presence, which of course there was.

One evening Jim O'Donnell knocked the door to see if Tom was home but as he was busy gathering vegetables from the allotment, Jim left a message with Patsy. It was from the Site Manager at Berkley Power Station saying that Tom was needed and that a new job was waiting for him, that of Site Foreman on double the old pay! Taking a deep breath, and inwardly thanking the Lord for his new found luck, Tom packed his bag and was gone the very next morning, leaving Patsy in tears of frustration and anger, feeling that once again money seemed to rule in his head.

"Sod those bloody bloodsuckers in Ireland," she cried out to him as he left through the front door.

Tom got into Jim O'Donnell's car, and they headed for his old digs in Mrs Brown's house in Thornbury, and then onto his new job at Berkley, and his new salary which would now keep both families going, or so he thought!

Chapter 2

Sally Smith

Sally Smith sat on a hard wooden bench in the Coroner's Court in Long Ashton, Bristol, tears flowing, and her head bowed with shame, while listening to the verdict at the inquest into her husband's death.

Her friends, Claire Cummings and Elaine sat either side of her, holding her hand while the Coroner read his report out to the people who were attending this sombre meeting. Harold Smith, it was decided, died an accidental death. He had fallen in the lounge, hitting his head as he fell, and suffering a massive brain injury and substantial blood loss. The paramedics were unable to help him, and he was pronounced dead at the scene. Harold's state of mind, and the massive quantity of alcohol he had consumed that day, were cited as the main reasons for his outrageous behaviour and it was decided that no further action would be taken in relation to his attack on the two children. Harold had no police record of any kind, not even a speeding ticket.

It was also determined that he had suffered a sudden breakdown, which had occurred because of the stresses and strains being placed on him at the council, where jobs and budgets were being cut, leaving him the bearer of the bad news, and despised by many. The fact that his wife was working long hours, coupled with the fostering of the two children meant that he could not cope mentally, and this pushed him over the edge.

The Coroner also told Sally that she was in no way to blame, and should not at any time feel responsible for Harold and his actions, as his mind was deranged at the time of his death. However, this did not make Sally feel any better, and Claire and Elaine hugged her in unison as the final verdict was read out. It was then that Sally fell to pieces, dissolving in her friends' arms, howling, finally letting out the hurt, pain and embarrassment this whole nasty matter had caused her.

Veronica was sat at the back of the Coroner's Court listening intently to everything. She had been Harold's personal prostitute for the last 25 years, and knew all about this evil man, sad thing was, Sally knew about her, and Harold's monthly visits to her house, but didn't know who she was or where she lived, and when his death was announced out of the blue in the Local Bristol Post the day after she had cancelled his appointment, when her mother had been taken suddenly ill, she felt it only right to sneek into the back of the court to try and find out what had exactly happened to him; what she heard made her feel totally sick inside and very scared; When the verdict was finally read out she said to herself, "Oh, God, you have absolutely no idea about this man," her thoughts running riot. She felt so sorry for his wife Sally who was now being helped out of the court by two ladies. Veronica suddenly felt that she was very lucky to have escaped the clutches of this man, and all of his crooked friends.

Three months later, the insurance company paid Sally, Harold's life insurance money. She was now free to do whatever she liked. Her psychic gifts were now starting to flow again, and she was even thinking of reading, and was planning to ask her lovely Megan to come and help, but something was making her feel uneasy. She had a funny feeling in her tummy all the time lately, and what was worrying her, was that it usually meant trouble. Where or when she did not know, but it was coming, of that she was sure.

Harold's money now meant that Sally was financially very comfortable. Harold's pension was also now being paid into her account on a monthly basis, which really meant that she did not have to work anymore. However, she was lonely, and missed Megan and Tinker and the lovely family life that she briefly shared with them, and would often burst into tears, cursing Harold for his behaviour and for breaking up her family dream. If it hadn't been for Claire and Elaine, her dear friends, who kept her going, she probably would have tried to end it all herself, that's how bad it had got for her just after Harold's death.

One night, while doing a nightshift at the local hospital, she sought out one of her friends, a lovely lady doctor called Winnie Wilkinson. It worried Sally very much that she was still having these terrible thoughts, and decided to have a quiet chat with her. After a couple of hours, Winnie totally reassured Sally that all she was going through was a healing process. It was perfectly normal to have those sorts of thoughts after such traumatic events and the sudden death of her husband, and she was strongly convinced that these thoughts would gradually leave her mind once her career was back on track, and she knew exactly where she was going with her life. She also suggested that a move might be a good thing, as still living in the house where her husband had attacked the children and then died, kept the brain recalling bad memories.

"You are so right, Winnie," she said to her smiling, "thank you." She kissed her on the cheek before leaving the doctor's office to head back to the ward, smiling as she walked down the corridor, and making a new plan in her head for the future.

Sally decided that moving house was the right thing to do. She was also very worried about Megan and Tinker. She felt that it was her duty to be on hand for them should they need her. God only knew that having to put up with a demon for a mother was one thing, but having to fight off the other one made family life even harder. She missed them so much and decided that being near them would also help her to move on.

The large family flat was put onto the market and it sold within a week, much to Sally's delight. A lovely family moving down from Sutton Coldfield fell in love with the flat immediately, and offered Sally her asking price.

"Thank you, Lord," she said out loud and looking skywards just after the family had left to contact their solicitor.

Sally in turn found her ideal house the very next day. While travelling through Whitchurch, she came across a small cul-de-sac in a little hamlet right on the outskirts, just 5 minutes' drive from the Murphy house, which made Sally smile.

"Just right, Sally," said Claire and Elaine in unison, as they viewed the house, walking through the rooms, taking in the atmosphere, and noting several things that needed doing.

"Needs updating," said Elaine.

"New carpets and a lick of paint!" commented Claire.

"Oh, you could convert this small room for your readings," they both said in unison, excitedly.

"Yes I agree, and I have the money to do it, thanks to Harold," said Sally smiling, turning to her two lovely friends, and hugging them both.

"Well what are you waiting for?" they again shouted at her this time laughing.

"Wait!" said Sally suddenly. "We have a visitor."

"Yes we do," said Claire, "it's Harold, love," she said looking at Sally worriedly.

"Oh, God no," cried out Sally.

"One moment, be calm," said Claire, vanishing into thin air, leaving Elaine and Sally holding onto one another in the hall, and looking around for their friend. With a puff of thin wispy smoke, Claire returned. "Okay, nothing to worry about, he likes the new home, and he was just making sure you were okay," she said looking at Sally, who had tears tumbling down her cheeks, and a frightened and worried look set on her face. "I have asked him to leave, and move on in to the light and leave you alone, which he has done."

"Oh thank you, Claire, I really don't want him around, it's my turn now; he had his chance."

"Come on," said Claire putting her arm around Sally's shoulder, "let's go and make an offer."

"Yes let's," Sally replied, wiping tears from her eyes as she left the house.

The name of the new house was Fernwood. Sally moved in 2 months later. The house contained one double and 2 medium sized bedrooms upstairs, with a very large and modern bathroom to service them all. Downstairs there was a very large kitchen diner. There was also a large, safe and enclosed south facing garden to the rear, along with a nice sized double garage to the side of the house, and 2 nice sized front living rooms at the front, overlooking a neat garden with a small lawn, and shrubs placed all around for colour.

Sally had the entire house painted, decorated and furnished to her liking within 6 weeks, Elaine and Claire staying over to help her. Claire's jobs included cleansing the house of any old remaining spirits who were connected to the old owners, so that her own psychic readings could take place without any interference, and the end result of all their hard work was a wonderful homely smart house.

"Thank you so much, my darlings, cheers," said Sally pouring them all a large glass of finest champagne. "I have a real home again."

"Here, here," her friends replied chinking their glasses in a toast.

All I need now is my little family around me again, Megan and Tinker, thought Sally.

"You will," said Claire winking to her as she sipped on her gently bubbling pink fizz with a big smile on her face.

Chapter 3

New School

That morning was no different than any other weekday: getting up, making soda bread, tidying the house ready for when their mother would return from work, making breakfast, and getting her brothers and sister up, dressed, fed and ready for school. Except somehow that day was different. She felt very sick, nervous, and hesitant, and all because it would be her very first day at her new secondary school, Haybury Comprehensive.

She had slept badly that night. The growling outside her window had annoyed her so much that for the first time, she had actually shouted at it to shut up, which then woke her sister and made matters worse. The baby's cry was louder than ever, which also gave her an uneasy feeling, so sleep that night was almost impossible, which in turn made her tetchy and tired come the morning.

"Oh sod!" she cried out as she leapt out of bed, and ran down the stairs to open the front door. "Sod it!" she cursed out loud; the blue tits had beaten her to the milk, piercing little holes through the foil to sip out the glorious creamy top of the milk, so beloved on the cereals and porridge by all, especially her mother. She had forgotten that the milkman always called early on a Monday morning, and suddenly remembered that her mother had popped into her bedroom earlier that morning before she went to work and whilst Megan was in a hazy sleep, reminding her to bring the milk in early.

That's another slap, she told herself inwardly and shuddered at the thought. "As if I haven't got enough to do today," she grunted.

Siblings up, washed and fed, it was time for everyone to dress for school. They gathered in the tiny kitchen, waiting for their uniforms to be handed down from the little line which ran above the cooker and dresser. The uniforms were hung there every night, pressed with love and pride by their mother and kept sparkling clean like military medals just waiting to be worn the next day.

Megan passed down the boys' uniforms first and they ran up to their bedroom to put theirs on. She and Trixie then stood in the kitchen in front of the open oven door, which was always lit on a cold morning, so they could dress in warmth. This always did the trick; the house was made of pre-formed concrete, and had no central heating, so this was a perfect solution to dressing in the cold.

Megan was proudly admiring her brand new school uniform, a rarity for her as her mother usually gave her second-hand or hand-me-down uniforms, when suddenly and without any warning, Trixie let out the most terrible scream that shot through Megan like a hot knife through butter and nearly dropped her on the spot.

"Argh," Trixie screamed out again, "get it off me, get it off me."

She was screaming in total fear, louder this time, and with that, fainted. Megan nearly fainted to, as a huge black hairy house spider was lying in wait inside of Trixie's school skirt, and in sheer surprise at being disturbed in its cosy lair, had bitten her on the leg. Both boys were now screaming, and charging down the hall after the monster that had attacked their beloved sister, squashing it unceremoniously as it tried in vain to flee.

Megan realised as she tried to comfort her unconscious sister, that something was very wrong. Trixie was a funny blue colour, and appeared to have trouble breathing, so she shouted out to the boys to stay with their sister while she ran next door to Mr & Mrs Winters to call the doctor.

Mr & Mrs Winters helped to look after the family by tending the allotment and garden while their father was away working. They were a lovely couple; both retired from the army, and both very enthusiastic about gardening, and loved the company of the family who lived next to them. Megan instantly told Mrs Winters what had happened and she immediately rang the local health centre.

Dr Williamson had just arrived at the local health centre in his beloved Volkswagen Camper van. He was near retirement age himself and was well known and loved for his interest in the wellbeing of underprivileged children in the area.

The receptionist, who had taken the telephone call from Mrs Winters rushed out into the car park and informed him of the immediate and very serious problem. Dr Williamson turned straight around and with all haste, drove to the house like a madman, fearing the worst. He knew this family: lovely children, bitch of a mother. If only his dear and loving wife Gwennie was alive now, he would try and adopt those kids he so admired. They could never have a family of their own, and so he kept himself busy, trying as much as possible to be in touch with the one thing he so wished had affected his life.

Trixie was in a state of allergic shock by the time Dr Williamson arrived, and the spider's bite was the size of a Jaffa cake, and nearly the same colour as well! She was struggling to breathe, and quite blue in colour. Megan and the boys were quite hysterical and crying now, not knowing how to help their little sister.

"What happened?" Dr Williamson shouted at them as he rushed in through the door.

"Massive spider bit her on the leg," a tearful Megan replied.

"Well done, Megan," he replied, "she must have an allergy to insect bites." He opened his bag and took out a very large syringe and needle, which made the boys scream even louder in sheer panic at the size of the needle in his hand. "Now, now," said Dr Williamson, as he carefully administered the adrenalin, "she will be fine now; we use this to counteract the venom which she is allergic to. Where's Mum?" he asked.

"Work," replied Megan.

"Right then, I am taking her with me to the surgery, she can stay there with me today no need for the hospital or the Social Services to know about this, and I can do some bloodwork and make sure she's better for school tomorrow." Looking around the sparse but clean and tidy house at the three spotless and smartly dressed children, his thoughts turned back to his Gwennie, knowing she would have swept them all up in her arms, and taken them home with her, had she been there. "Off to school then you three, and don't worry, I will telephone the schools and let them know why you are late on the first day back. I will also speak with Mum when she gets home, and don't worry, Trixie will be fine now," he said lifting little Trixie up in his arms and walking out to his camper van, gently laying her on the bench at the back, and wrapping her in a blanket to keep her warm until he reached the surgery. "Go on now, go to school, she will be fine, I promise, and you are not in any trouble," and with that he got into his van and drove carefully up the road.

It was a long walk to the new school. Shamus, Megan's little brother was still at her old school, so that made it easy for him. The new headmistress was Elaine Brent, who came with sparkling credentials, vowing to improve standards, and put right all that was wrong that had now given the school such a bad name. A new school nurse had also been appointed who had come from the local doctors' surgery. Her name was Lindsay Blue. Several new teachers had also been appointed but best of all they now had an advisory governor, which Megan thought was brilliant news. Together they were set to get the school back on track, and meet all the School Board's standards within the next year.

Shame they couldn't do that when I was there, Megan thought. But this was a new day, and a new start, she was telling herself as she tried to keep up with Tinker as they made their way to Haybury, which was some 3 miles away, and a good 40 minute walk.

It was the size of the school which made Megan's jaw drop. She and Tinker had arrived very late, and lessons were well under way. It was now half past ten, and they were walking as fast as their little legs would carry them, across the school playing fields and heading towards the main building, and up to the school offices.

Oh what a disaster, Megan was thinking as they made their way into the front of the school, and up the large spiral staircase which serviced all four floors of the building. The offices, thank goodness, were on the first floor and they arrived flushed of face, and nervous about the reception awaiting them.

The headmaster's door was large, and painted bright green, with big brass lettering on the front. 'Headmaster, Mr Edward Scott', it said. Two young ladies were chatting at the reception desk, and another older lady was directing one of the secretaries to take mail to the various recipients on the front of the letters she had in her hand.

The headmaster's door opened. "Ah, you must be Megan," said a very large and well-dressed man who emerged from the room. "Good morning, Tinker," he smiled at her brother.

"Good morning, sir," Tinker replied.

"Well I gather you have all had quite a morning, but it ended well. Your sister is fine by the way; I've just had Dr Williamson on the phone. Well done, Megan for acting so fast. She's awake now, and being looked after by the nurses at the surgery. He is keeping her for the day, and she will be home by the time you two get back later. Right then, Tinker you know where you are going? Don't worry; I have already spoken to your teacher. Do you have your timetable?" he asked.

"Yes, sir."

"Very well then, off you go. Megan you follow me," and with that, he headed down the corridor, back down the stairs, and along another long corridor, which headed towards the end of the building on the bottom floor.

They arrived at the end of the corridor outside a large door which had the words 'Home Economics Dept.' in large letters above it. He handed Megan a weekly rotation sheet which explained what lessons she had, and which classrooms to attend every day of the week.

"You will report to room 2a in building 4 every morning for registration, and then into the main hall for assembly every Friday morning. You must find your own way to your lessons; it's all marked out on the map. And you will be in different classrooms for different lessons, it's quite clear. Any questions?" he asked.

"No," Megan replied feeling bewildered, but knowing that Tinker would help her out in her first week.

"Don't worry you will soon pick it up," he told her. "Now where are we, ah yes, it's 11am, so on your timetable it's Home Economics, always here, the kitchens are inside, and Mrs Evershott is your teacher. She's a lovely lady and a brilliant cook and seamstress, you two will get on very well. I gather you are also a very good cook. Dr Williamson spoke very highly of you. You look after your brothers and sister while Mum and Dad are working. Well done, that takes some doing, but you will have to work hard here, and work at your studies. Extra help is available if you need it, Megan, do you understand?" She nodded and smiled back at him. "Right, let's get you in class," he said as he opened the door and walked across the pristine kitchen to where the students were gathered in front of a very large blackboard.

"Hello, Mrs Evershott," he called out, and from behind the blackboard, a small, red haired lady with gold rimmed glasses appeared.

"Good morning, Headmaster," she replied.

"This is Megan Murphy."

"Well thank you, Headmaster. Good morning, Megan, we have heard a lot about you, welcome to the Home Economics Department and your classmates. Everyone say hello to Megan," she firmly demanded.

"Hello, Megan!" they all called out in unison, and with that, Mrs Evershott took Megan by the hand and showed her an empty desk and chair, which she could sit at.

"Have a good day, everyone," Mr Scott waved as he turned and left the classroom. He turned and smiled at Megan. "Remember, Megan, if you need anything please come and ask, okay?" and gave a cheeky wink at Mrs Evershott, who instantly flushed up bright red from her neck to the top of her head.

Oh my! she gasped inwardly.

He was secretly giggling to himself as he left the classroom. He knew she had a little crush on him and he loved teasing her, always congratulating her on her dress, and her hair, which made an old spinster feel really good.

"Oh yes," Mrs Evershott said to herself, "it's going to be a good day today. Excuse me," she said to a very large black and gold angel she squeezed past that was looking over Megan's shoulder at something she was writing. *Oh Sally was right, we really do have someone special this term, I must ring and thank her.*

Mrs Jean Evershott was a really lovely lady, who reminded Megan of her dearest friend and second mother, Sally Smith, who she thought about quite a lot.

"I have heard a lot about you, Megan," she said, "are you very interested in cooking?" she asked.

"Yes I cook for my two brothers and sister when Mum and Dad are working."

"What!" exclaimed the rest of the class.

"Our mums do everything. I can't even cook toast," shouted out a small blonde haired girl in the corner called Eva.

"Not even a boiled egg," shouted another girl with long frizzy hair, called Janet.

"No nothing," 3 others cried out all laughing, which made Megan feel right at home and she smiled at them all.

"Well you will with me. By the end of the first term, you will all start to look after yourselves, and by the time you leave you will all have good housekeeping skills, which will look after you all for the rest of your lives, and there will be no exceptions, understand?" she said loudly to them all.

"Yes, Mrs Evershott," they all replied giggling loudly, and bursting into laughter.

"Oh, Lord thank you," Megan said quietly to herself, saying a quick prayer as another angel appeared at her side.

"Enjoy," said the angel, "you are very safe here."

Mrs Evershott gasped at the sight of the beautiful gold and cream angel who was conversing with Megan, and just for a moment, she could not think or move. "Oh, God I need a cup of tea. Right, everyone!" she cried out. "Let's get to the stoves," and with that Megan's first lesson in her new school had begun.

The day flew by: English, maths – oh she so struggled with maths. Having number blindness was a real problem, but she struggled on as best she could, and then history. Oh joy! She had loved every minute, but as soon as the bell rang to signal the end of the day, she packed her beloved brown leather satchel with all the new books she had acquired. The satchel now seemed to weigh double. She then made her way across the playing fields to take the shortcut up past the new Catholic church she sometimes attended, down through the posh housing estate, down to the horses' field, and up across the train line by the old guard's hut. She rarely went this way as it was muddy most days, and when playing out with friends in this area, as they often did, she always got muddy and mud was not a thing to take home to her house, unless you wanted a slap. But Megan was worried, and wanted to get home to find out how Trixie was, and this short cut would gain her twenty minutes.

Dr Williamson's camper van was parked outside their house, and Megan felt her stomach churn when she saw it and without stopping to think about anything else, she made her way up the road to the front gate. The front door suddenly opened and Dr Williamson emerged.

"Ah, Megan, there she is the little angel who saved your life," he said turning and looking at little Trixie, who was now standing next to her mother. Her mother glowered big nasty looking green eyes at her. "Megan," Dr Williamson looked at her and asked, "how do you feel about coming with me and my group twice a week to swim and do gymnastics? I would pick you up with the other boys and girls who come along, and I would bring you home safe and sound. It's every Tuesday and Thursday night 6.30 till 8.30." Megan looked at her mother. "Megan," said Dr Williamson looking directly at her mother, "would you like to come along?"

"Yes, thank you," replied Megan.

"Right then, that's sorted. I will pick you up 6.30 sharp tomorrow evening for swimming.

"Goodbye," he called out as he was walking down the front path to his camper van which was parked outside. He got in and drove off down the road.

"Trix you okay?" asked Megan.

"Yes fine really, apparently I have had an allergic reaction and possibly I will have to be careful with any insect bite in the future, especially wasp and bee stings. I will know more when Mum takes me to the hospital for some more tests."

A sharp slap across the rear of the head shocked Megan back into reality.

"Ow, what's that for?" cried a distraught Megan.

"For letting the bloody birds get into the milk, especially after I came into your bedroom and told you to be up for the milkman before I left this morning," her mum screamed at her. "Now get upstairs and get out of that uniform, and get your homework done, tea is at six."

Megan ran upstairs tears blurring her vision. "Bloody cow bag," she cried to herself, "what else is she going to do tonight?" She took off her uniform, folding it precisely, and got into her clean play clothes. At least today at school she had not looked any different to any other student. Her new school uniform of which she was really proud, made her smile, and she repeatedly thanked the angels and the universe until Michael, her main angel appeared and told her to stop it, it was fine, just enjoy school.

The evening meal was homemade quiche with a baked potato, garden salad, and egg mayonnaise, which if there was any left over, would be put into the sandwiches for school the next day. Pudding was a baked apple filled with sweet mincemeat and thick cream. Heaven!

The waft of cooking food crept up the stairs, as they were all finishing their homework before coming down for tea. The aroma teased their hungry bellies as they sat and wrote faster and faster making sure everything was finished, so that they could go out and play for an hour when tea was over.

As soon as tea was finished, Megan helped her mother wash-up, and tidy, and then headed for the bottom of the garden where her fairies lived. The other kids were down at the playground, but Megan wanted to spend some time with her little friends who were such a big part of her life. She loved playing with them, teasing them and helping them with their chores. This was her idea of heaven. Time passed quickly when she played with her little friends. Running down the garden path she called out in anticipation, which she usually did, and normally they would respond immediately, flying all around her like a swarm of bees, excited to see her.

"Amberley, Queen Ella, Josh, Brightness, Star!"

But nothing happened and the fairies didn't appear. She arrived at the little nest she had built for them and in which they lived in her garden, but it was deserted. Again and again she called to them, but they did not appear.

What she did not realise was, they had gone, gone to hide away, away from the nasty demon they had seen, they suddenly didn't feel safe, and when the Fairies didn't feel safe you knew you had trouble!

In the background she heard a growl, a wolf like growl. She hesitated, stopped and looked around. Her spine tingled and again she called out to them but still there was nothing. The growl was coming nearer. Her spine tingled again, but harder this time. She felt the little bumps in the back of her neck rise, her neck thicken, and small fangs appeared, slowly dropping into her mouth.

"Oh, Lord, something or someone is very wrong here, please help, where have all my fairies gone?" she asked.

Once again, the growl came closer.

"Megan," Michael the angel suddenly appeared, "time for you to go."

"Megan!" her mother's voice rang out from the kitchen.

"Coming," replied Megan. She turned and in the distance spotted a pair of orange eyes looking straight at her.

"Go, child," Michael ordered, and she turned and ran back into the kitchen where her mother waited.

"Problem?" asked her mother.

"No nothing," she replied running upstairs to look out of her bedroom window. But she couldn't see anything. Feeling unsure and quite bewildered, she called to Michael.

"Michael are you there?" she quietly asked out loud, hoping for a response, but there was no reply. "Oh sod it." Something was happening or would happen soon, she was sure of it, she could feel it, sense it. Things were about to change in a big way!

Chapter 4

Nine months on

It was now almost 9 months since Megan had started in her new school, Haybury Comprehensive, and things were going well. Her very first cooking exam was looming, and she was starting to feel increasingly worried. This would be the first of 4 exams that she would take over the next 2 years, and at the end of it, she should have attained an O' Level in Home Economics and advanced cookery.

Her father never seemed to be home, making her mother Patsy really miserable. Money was tight, and most worrying of all Megan needed £2 to buy the ingredients for the exam, but £2 was a fortune to her family, and her head was spinning, trying to fathom out ways of attaining that very valuable amount.

The other problem looming in the very near future was of course Bonfire Night. It was a time of celebration when the whole street gathered together and enjoyed themselves. This once a year event was always very special, and much loved by everyone. A great deal of hard work was needed to ensure that it met the crowd's expectations, which actually it always did, but this year it felt different, and Megan really did not know why.

Large brown envelopes were arriving weekly from the Council Housing Department, and she knew her mother was worried. One evening she spied over her mother's shoulder as she was sat on her stool in the kitchen, and fleetingly saw the words 'debt collector', and 'eviction'. No wonder Patsy was miserable and worried.

God! Where would we all go if we were thrown out? she wondered.

The other thing that was worrying her was that she was absolutely sure that her mother was paying the rent every week, always leaving for the rent office with notes stuffed in the brown rent book, ready to pay, so what was the problem, she constantly questioned? Megan herself started to worry, which of course didn't help at all, and just to top it all off, there was some sort of demon trouble about. She could sense it, almost smell it, like thick foggy treacle falling from the sky above, covering all of them, and trying to block their senses.

Thank God, Sally had moved nearer and Megan hoped that perhaps she might get back in touch, and might be able to help. She often wondered how best to get in contact with her, and sometimes asked Michael and his angels who constantly stood guard in her bedroom, but they never seemed to reply. Perhaps the real answer was about to be revealed! Never a truer word thought or spoken…

Chapter 5

Bright yellow door

The residents of the estate had all received a letter from the council earlier that year informing them that the time had come, as it did every 5 years, for everyone to have their front and back doors, and their garden gate, along with all the window frames, painted. This was an exciting time for all the council tenants. At this moment in time, most of their doors were cracked and peeling and very drab, so were the matching front garden gates, not to mention the cracking, peeling window frames. Yes, the whole estate badly needed a facelift and thank goodness it was coming!

Fred Mathews was a council man, through and through. He had started his working life with Bristol Council when he was a mere 16 years old, working as a tea lad and a gofer, with the rubbish and waste department, clearing out houses and taking all the unwanted furniture and rubbish to the local tip. Twenty-five years later, he had made his way right to the top and was now management, having his own teams of decorators and carpenters which the council duly employed.

The workmen that were available to him for this particular project had been split into two teams. Fifty would work alongside him, and concentrate on the repainting of the estate, and with over 400 houses on the list, they would most certainly have their work cut out, as the contract had to be finished in 3 months. The other 50 painters, decorators and carpenters would carry on doing the regular day to day jobs which the council tenants needed doing. That could be anything from fitting a new door, to a complete redecoration of a house after a tenant had moved, died or been evicted, making it ready, and spick and span for the eager new occupier. He was also responsible for the decorating of all the new homes that the council were building at the moment.

There would always be work for the decorators, it was of course, a totally ongoing job, and Fred Mathews was at the top of his game. At the tender age of 18 he had been taken under the wing of an old boy that he was working alongside. Teddy, as he was known, was a brilliant decorator, manager, and all round handyman. He was an expert in almost everything, and he became a dear friend and teacher to Fred, who sucked all his information in like a sponge. As he got older, and rose in the ranks, Fred used every little piece of stashed away information to finally get him to where he wanted to be, and now there he was, in charge of them all, with over 100 staff. He hired them and of course, fired them, and he knew absolutely every single member of his team, all their specialties, their faults, who was good at certain jobs, and who would be better at another, and with a tight budget, and short deadline to meet (3 months) he chose his team carefully. He had in his opinion, the best lads for the job in hand here, lads who would put their whole heart and soul into the job, get their heads down, and get on with it, without wasting precious time and money. Overtime would be limited to one hour per day, at least until the end of the contract when they would work flat out, doing whatever it took to get the job finished on time and within budget.

Four large metal containers, normally used for shipping goods abroad, were deposited down at the end of the street, near the allotments, on the waste ground. Two would be filled with the precious paint and other stock that would be needed to service all 400 homes on the estate, and the other two containers would act as an office, changing rooms for the men, and of course, the very badly needed staff tea rooms. The local police were informed of the presence of the council, and of course the two loaded containers of stock, and Sergeant William Brown, the newly promoted sergeant in the force, and his team, would be informed and make regular evening rounds, checking on the containers to ensure that they were secured and that no precious stock went missing.

It was Fred's job to allocate a painter to each house. Each house would have a specific job sheet, telling the painter exactly what work needed to be done right down to how bad the condition of the doors, gate and window frames were. Any filler that was needed was noted, what primer to use, and what colour the occupant had chosen, and more importantly, how long he had to complete the job.

Exactly one week before the whole project was due to commence, Fred started knocking on all the doors on the estate. He started at the very end of the estate, which was the cul-de-sac down by the golf course, overlooking the lovely fields which were full of wild flowers, butterflies and brightly coloured insects. He always sighed when working around this part of the estate as it was truly breathtaking; a real nice piece of estate.

This could one day be private, and very much sought after, he thought to himself as he knocked the door of the house at the end, and was greeted by a very old lady, who invited him in to inspect the doors, gate and window frames, once she had seen his identity card. She watched him closely as he made notes on his clipboard and then left, only to knock on the house next door, but not before asking her the most important question of all.

"What colour would you like your two doors and front gate painted?"

The choice that was on offer from the council was, a lovely deep blood red, a lovely deep navy blue, a dark emerald green, and a bright golden buttercup yellow.

Fred was making good progress, and all of the 40 occupants he had knocked on so far had been in, and apart from one house whose doors were really in a bad state, one door needing to be completely replaced, it was all good. He was feeling confident that he would get the job done without any hassle, and best of all, almost all of them had chosen red and blue for their doors and gates, with only a couple now starting to choose the green. His spirits were high, as he realised that he could now renegotiate the price of the paint with the supplier. It was now mostly just red and blue that he would need to order in bulk, and this would help his budget, keep everything in line and especially on target.

He rubbed his hands together, already starting to feel the money in his grasp. Every time a project he was asked to do came in on time, and especially under budget, he received a well-earned bonus cheque, and on today's surveying, this bonus should be a really good one. He visualised himself and his lovely wife on the beach in Alicante, cold beer in his hand, his wife happy, (thank God) and a large jug of Sangria next to her sunbed.

Oh yes, Alicante! Here we come.

A week later, he had nearly finished going around the estate, inspecting all of the houses, and putting the last bits of the jobs needed to be done on the job sheets for the men to start on in just a couple of days.

There were just 10 houses left. Fred walked up and down the street viewing the outside of the houses, making notes on them all, and commenting on each job sheet so each workman knew exactly what he was telling them.

The house he was currently looking at belonged to Audrey Collings. It was right next door to the Murphy house. She had only just moved in and was already busy decorating the inside of the house herself. As the road nosey, nothing passed her by and she was constantly looking out of the window, watching everything and anybody that passed, and of course, always taking her own personal notes, which she could then relay to her friends and family by telephone.

She noticed this handsome man straightaway, and was thrilled, and very excited to see Fred starting to walk down her front garden path. She didn't wait for him to knock on the door, choosing instead to open it very wide, with a huge, sexy and seductive smile. She was sexually attracted to this tall well-built, red haired man. Her blouse front had been pulled down meaning that her ample, untouched swellings were well in sight. Her lipstick had been quickly and freshly applied and she was fluttering her big spider-like false eyelashes. She was excited by this male hunk, who looked as if he liked to work with his hands, and she immediately started having naughty thoughts about him, smiling even wider as he approached.

"Hello, who are you?" she asked him, intrigued.

"Oh, I am Fred Mathews, here on behalf of the council," he said showing her his card. "We are starting work here next week, repainting all front and back doors, garden gates, and all your window frames, although actually, yours don't look too bad at all," he commented looking around. "Can I just pop round the back to see the back door and windows?" he asked quickly, realising this lonely cougar was looking him up and down, digesting him and preparing to strike. He returned within 30 seconds. "All done, just as I thought, not much work needed here, he'll be finished within a few days," he told her.

"Who will?" she asked with a raised excited voice.

"Oh sorry," he replied, "each house will be allocated its own painter and decorator, who will report to me, and I will promise to oversee everything personally, until he has finished the job to your satisfaction, and may I add…"

"Oh!" exclaimed Audrey cutting him short, and now very excited at the prospect of a workman all of her own, who she could look after, lavish with her attention, tea, coffee, sandwiches, and maybe sex! Oh yes, perhaps she could get him into bed to do wonderful things with her body, which she could only imagine now on her long lonely nights in her big brass bed, whilst being totally frustrated seeing that fabulous hunk Tom Murphy who she constantly fantasised about. He lived next door with the family from hell or at least that's what she had named them. But never mind, this was a really exciting time, and she was suddenly away with the fairies.

"Hello!" Fred called out bringing her back to reality, a flush to his face. "What colour do you want for your doors and gate?" he asked.

28

"Green," she replied, "yes green!"

"The red and blue are better, everyone is choosing those," he said frantically trying to change her mind, whilst thinking about his bonus and holiday in Alicante.

"No, I want green," she replied forcefully.

Damn and blast it! he thought, looking towards her and tipping his hat, before turning and walking down the path. "Bloody sod it. Sod it! This is going to start to cost me," he grumbled to himself as he opened the gate to the Murphy house.

Patsy was in the kitchen, making her beloved mother's old recipe of bread pudding. It was one the family loved and ate with relish when they smelled it slowly cooking in the oven. The charismatic sweet spicy smell would waft around the house, teasing their senses and their rumbling tummies, all in eager anticipation of this most delicious humble dish.

She had saved all the scraps of bread throughout the week, both white and brown; it didn't really matter what colour bread you used, as it would all be mashed up together, and leftovers were absolutely perfect for this recipe.

She had started off the process the night before, after the children had gone to bed, and she was all alone down in her little kitchen, with only the radio, the nightly play and her cup of something for company. She soaked the mixed dried fruit and peel in strong tea, which she would drain off in the morning, leaving the fruit deliciously plump and moist, just ready to use.

That morning, after the children had gone to school, with only the ironing to do, she set about the bread pudding, tearing all the pieces of leftover bread into little chunks and putting it all into a large mixing bowl. She then added the plump fruit, the zest of an orange and lemon, and milk, before scrunching it all together with her hands. She mixed everything well, completely breaking up the bread, squeezing extra hard at times when little thoughts of that evil Father Quinn came into her mind. Just for a moment she imagined that she was throttling the very life out of him with a satisfied smile on her face, but she suddenly came out of her daydreaming, realising that her hand had turned blue with the pressure that she had applied to the mashed bread and fruit she was holding. She took a deep breath, stopped and looked around, realising she was still in the kitchen with her hand in a large bowl of mashed up bread and fruit, and came back to reality. She added the beaten eggs and Muscovado sugar, and gave it all a good loving stir, and left it to soak for about 15 minutes while she set about greasing the bread pudding tin.

Her attention was suddenly caught by noises coming from the back of the house.

Peering out of her small kitchen window, she realised that it was voices she heard, and they were coming from next door. She noticed a tall plump red haired man inspecting the windows and doors of Audrey Collings' house.

Then a couple of minutes later he started walking down the garden path towards Patsy's front door, still looking down at his clipboard and making notes as he went. Just as he was about to knock on the faded door, a terrible feeling of sickness came over him making him stop for a moment, and hold on to the side of the garden hedge to support himself while he was heaving and almost retching. He steadied himself, and took a deep breath. Patsy had been quietly watching him from behind the thick net curtains in the front room window, smiling as he retched and turned blue. The sickness passed as quickly as it had arrived, and apparently now feeling a little better and more composed, the man knocked on her door.

Patsy opened the door and instantly he could hear a low growl from somewhere behind her. He instinctively stepped back, not wanting to be bitten again by another dog. It had been bad enough last time. He had been cornered in a little bungalow by a massive Golden Retriever which had tried to bite his arm off. He shuddered at the thought and quickly pushed it to one side and smiled at this tall, blonde, alluring and green eyed lady.

"Hello, I'm Fred Mathews from the council. We are starting a repainting programme next week for all of the council tenants on the estate and I've just come to look at your windows and doors for the job sheet if that's okay?" he asked her, while she looked him up and down, her big green eyes flashing.

"You can go around the back through the alleyway," she replied with a quiet voice, closing the front door. Fred saw the alley and was relieved not to be going through the house and facing that massive sounding dog. The back gate, which led into the back garden and the kitchen door, was open. He quickly inspected the back door, which once again was in very good condition. So too were the window sills and frames.

They won't take much work, he thought happily. Turning around he left the back garden, going back through the alleyway, and again knocked on the front door. Patsy was waiting for the knock and opened the door.

"Yes?" she asked him.

"Sorry, love, forgot to ask you, what colour do you want, red or blue?" he asked writing on his clipboard and not looking up at her.

"Yellow," she replied.

"Oh no, no, you can't have yellow," he replied sternly, quite cross at the thought.

The dog started to growl louder, and once again, he started feeling really sick.

"Yellow," she said again, gently, but firmly.

"I just told you, no one else has chosen yellow; now is it red or blue?" he replied forcefully, trying not to retch in front of her and feeling absolutely terrible. He had also noticed that Patsy's eyes were glowing really bright green. Bile was starting to rise in his throat and the dog was seemingly coming towards him judging by the loudness of the growl.

"Yellow," Patsy once again said, still looking at him.

Fred was shaking and sweating, retching and heaving. His breathing was deep and forceful and his head was spinning. He felt like he was about to pass out.

Patsy watched expressionless and silent.

Fred felt terrible and a pain shot through his head.

"Yellow," she repeated.

"Yellow," agreed Fred, scribbling on his clipboard, before turning and staggering down the garden path, closing the gate behind him, and heading for his car which was parked up the road. He was going straight home he decided as he staggered along the pavement. However, he instantly felt better once he had walked away from the house, and as suddenly as his symptoms had started, they were gone. He sat in his car and asked himself what had just happened back there, with that woman with the big green eyes, and the growling dog. Unsure, he decided to call it a day; he only had 8 houses left to do which he could finish tomorrow. He would go home and make an appointment to see his doctor just for a check-up, and make sure that at this important point with the painting contract about start, he wasn't going down with something.

By the time she got back into the kitchen the oven was at the right temperature. Patsy melted 3 ounces of butter in a small pan, and poured it into the bread mixture. The thought of the yellow door and front garden gate made her smile as she quickly worked, popping the complete mixture into the large tin, sprinkling it with brown sugar before putting it into the oven for about one and a half hours until firm. She would check on it every thirty minutes to make sure that it wasn't burning, and if it did, she could cover it with a butter paper until done.

Once cooked it would be cut into large finger bars, delicious sweet and spicy chunks of bread, that were lovely served warm with a cup of tea. Cold it would last a few days sealed in a clean biscuit tin, that's if it was allowed to.

As soon as the children came in from school that day, the tell-tale aroma of the bread pudding got them even more excited than the news about the doors and gate being painted. Four hungry children enjoyed warm bread pudding with their tea and toast that evening and everyone was satiated.

Dr Baxter was Fred's usual doctor. Old school, he had given all of his life to being a GP and a very good and renowned one he was too. He qualified at the age of 25, and was now just over 60, and due to retire within the next year.

"Hello, Fred what can I do for you today?" he asked him as he walked into his surgery.

Fred went into detail of what had happened to him that morning, and also about the new 3 month contract to paint the estate, and how his bonus relied on it, and how of course he couldn't afford to be off sick, especially now at this important stage.

Dr Baxter did all the usual routine examinations on Fred, even taking samples of blood to send away, but after a thorough going over, he could find absolutely nothing wrong with him, and gave him a clean bill of health. Confused and now slightly worried that he was losing his marbles, especially as he had agreed to allow Patsy Murphy to have yellow as her colour, he was babbling on as the doctor cleared away his instruments.

"Patsy Murphy's house?" asked Dr Baxter stopping Fred's continuing outburst.

"Yes, the Murphy house, that's where I was when I fell ill," he replied.

Dr Baxter burst out laughing. He knew all the Murphy family and used to be Patsy's doctor until a newly qualified mental health GP started at the practice. He recalled all the scary stories that surrounded the Murphy family, especially the house, and remembered well the 3 day birth of the eldest girl child, and how the doctor who attended felt exactly the same way in that house.

"Fred you are not ill, it's the house, it's said to be very haunted. My advice is, get that house done as quickly as possible, and don't go inside." He quickly told him all that he knew and what had been reported.

Fred left Dr Baxter's surgery relieved he wasn't ill, but started worrying about how he was going to handle getting that house done as fast as possible. Of all the 400 houses it was the only one which was going to be painted yellow. He decided to buy the yellow paint himself, enough just for her house, as this wouldn't affect his bonus whereas if he had to buy in a bulk amount of paint that wouldn't be used, it would. He would then be able to haggle for a better price on the other 3 colours, so saving him money on his budget, which would result in a better bonus.

The following week the council started its re-painting job on the estate. Patsy heard a knock at the front door. The children had gone to school, and she had just finished washing-up the breakfast dishes. She opened the door. Fred Mathews stood outside, feeling and looking quite nervous.

"Hello, Mrs Murphy, we've come to start the re-painting. The boys here will have it done as fast as possible, hopefully in the next couple of days," he said turning and showing Patsy the 6 workmen queuing up on the garden path. All the other houses had just one workman each, but Fred was determined to get this house done fast. The low growl of the large dog could be heard from somewhere inside the house, and Fred once again started to feel very sick. "Right, lads off we go, quick as possible please, and oh, do a good job, I don't want to come back here in a hurry," he quietly commented to them, passing over the filler, primer and 2 large pots of bright yellow paint.

Chapter 6

Dr Darrell Williamson

Dr Darrell Williamson at the age of 60 was now nearing retirement. Born in the city of Bristol, he had two lovely parents. His mother Alice was a housekeeper to a very large and wealthy family in Clifton, and his father who was called Edward was an insurance and loan salesman, working for a local firm, which specialised in door to door collections, and targeted council tenants who always seemed to struggle with house insurance, and more importantly, paying their bills.

They were a happy family; they lived in a large top floor flat on Durdham Downs, right at the top of Whiteladies Road, and not far from the now very famous Bristol Zoo. The flat was homely and welcoming, always clean and tidy, and Darrell always thanked the Lord for the view from his bedroom window when he went to sleep at night. The Clifton suspension bridge was a most amazing bridge and was built by none other than Isambard Kingdom Brunel. Most nights it was lit up by a thousand bulbs, a spectacle most people would never see. When Darrell's father gave him a camera on his 10th birthday, it was the first thing he ever photographed, and from that point onwards, photography would always be a love in his life.

His mother Alice worked very long hours. The family she worked for were very demanding, but paid her well, so most of her precious time was spent looking after the family who had 6 very demanding children, not really leaving her much time for her own. It was very quickly decided that Edward would take on the maternal duties as far as Darrell was concerned. Edward worked flexible hours, so he could easily work around his precious son, who he was very proud of.

Darrell went to a local school at the edge of Westbury-on-Trym, called Greenway, which specialised in athletics, gymnastics, rugby and football. Edward would take his son to school every day, leaving him to make his way home on the bus, but was always at hand when he needed to go to athletics or

34

gymnastics training. Therefore, although his mother worked long hours, and he didn't really get to see much of her, he never lacked love or attention, and flourished, getting really good grades at school and rising to county standard on the athletics track.

He was quite a loner at school, and many of his chums and classmates called him a nerd and a swot. He actually was neither. What he was doing was making sure that he would have enough qualifications when he left to do the one thing that he had set his mind and his heart on doing, much to the amazement of his parents, and that was to be a doctor. He quickly got a student's placement at Bristol School of Medicine, and he worked not far away at the Bristol Royal Infirmary as a student, rising to a junior doctor when he passed his first set of exams after five years of hard slog and long hours. He absolutely loved every moment, but often found himself wondering what on earth he ever would have done with his life, had he never made the grade. He needn't have worried however, as he found his specialty the very first day he set foot in the Bristol Children's Hospital at the top of St Michael's Hill. From that day onwards he had decided that he would specialise in Paediatrics, and children, and 10 long years later, he was a fully qualified doctor, and got his first job as a GP and Paediatrician in a small local suburb of Bristol called Henbury.

He also met his betrothed at the hospital, a girl called Gwendoline Phillips, who was a pretty and bright staff nurse with long blonde hair, big blue eyes, and a sexy smile. Long lonely nights attending the sick had brought them together, making them a great team, whether they were in or out of the hospital. Just before he took up his new post, they married and had a short honeymoon on the Isle of Wight, before moving into a rented flat in Henbury for 2 years, before finally setting up home in a small semi-detached house on the Wells Road, just on the outskirts of Whitchurch. He had been offered and taken a job at a very new and modern health centre just some 3 miles away in Stockvale. Darrell specialised in children; after all, he was a fully qualified paediatrician and specialist in child medicine, and here at this new health centre he would be kept very busy, having plenty of patients.

Stockvale had a large population of the poorer council tenants in Bristol and he quickly found out that quite a few were actually on the 'at risk' register, and he now realised that he would really have his work cut out. He relished the challenge of helping to improve the children's lives and health, especially their mental health. Over the years he became quite famous and families would wait for hours to see him in his surgery, hanging on to his every word and advice, always knowing he had the best in mind for their children. He was so well respected, that he started to work closely with the NSPCC and the local Social Services, and found himself being pulled in all directions as there were so many deserving and needy children that required his attention. He loved every moment of it, putting his heart and soul into his work and always saying a little prayer of thanks when a good move worked out, sometimes for the family, but usually for the neediest of children.

The sad part of his life was that his beloved wife Gwenn could never conceive. Despite private consultations, and a couple of operations, it just never happened for them. It was a void in their lives that always seemed to call out to them. To hide their despair and disappointment from each other, they both buried themselves in their work at the surgery. Gwennie was now Senior Sister in the treatment room, whilst Darrell kept busy with daily surgeries, and of course, they both worked really closely with the charities that specialised in underprivileged and disabled children. It seemed that their whole world was work, work work, but then when Gwennie suddenly collapsed one day at the surgery with a massive stroke and died instantly, he suddenly found himself very much alone. Both of his parents had died some years before, and with only a few distant relatives living up in Scotland which was at the other end of the country, loneliness quickly set in.

To keep the loneliness at bay, his mind active, and trying hard not to miss Gwennie, he started up a club. He would run it two evenings a week, Tuesday nights would be swimming at the Knowle swimming pool, and Thursday nights would be gymnastics and PE at St Brendon's School in Brislington. As he worked alongside the various charities, Social Services and the NSPCC, he quickly developed himself a nice little bunch of underprivileged children, he could dote on. He made sure that they had some much needed love and attention, often finding himself in tears as he drove away from the house where he had dropped the child back to after that night's activities, knowing what an awful situation and family he or she would be returning to.

His routine was to pick them all up between 6 and 6.30pm. They would then arrive at the pool or the gym by 7pm, always to be dropped off at home by 8.30, but not until after he had given them all a teaspoon of honey, a Haliborange chewy vitamin tablet, and any cough or cold medicine they needed. He also made sure they all had a hot cup of Baxter's oxtail soup from several large thermoses he kept in the back of the caravanette, and a cheese sandwich, which he always made fresh that day.

Now nearing 60, and his precious, but never forgotten Gwennie gone 10 years ago, he was starting to feel tired. He worked 7 days a week out of choice, and when the offer of retirement came his way, it started to look very appealing, and he kept it at the back of his mind.

It wasn't until the episode with Trixie Murphy and the spider bite, that he asked himself why he had never thought to include the Murphy children in his weekly club. Little Trixie had more than spilled the beans that particular day when he cared for her in the surgery as she recovered. The four surgery nurses had taken it in turns doing their observations every hour, taking blood and feeding her until she felt better, talking to her all the time, and learning all about her vicious mother, and how she had always hated and bullied Megan. The whole surgery knew about Megan's bullying and it was still being talked about now. He had read Patsy's notes and knew about the postnatal depression, and violent outbursts, and decided that day he would squeeze another needy child into the van for the clubs. It simply meant another can of Baxter's soup to be warmed, and another cheese sandwich to be made.

Patsy was not keen on letting Megan go to Dr Williamson's clubs, as it would mean another nose looking into her business, and another eye being kept on her, and that was the last thing she needed, she thought, as he asked her when depositing a well recovered Trixie back that afternoon after surgery. He knew that the rest of the children would be home from school any minute, and had kept her chatting until Megan came through the gate with a terribly worried look on her face.

She started at the swimming club the very next night, being picked up in the camper van right outside her front door at 6.30 sharp and being deposited back at 8.30 after having a lovely and much needed lesson to learn to swim. She had loved being sat in the back of the van afterwards, chatting and laughing with all the other children and enjoying the hot oxtail soup, and cheese sandwiches. Darrell was really disappointed when Megan told him she could only attend the swimming lesson on a Tuesday, and not the gym, and that she could only attend once a fortnight, as she had to look after her brothers and sister on a Tuesday and Thursday when her mother worked a late shift. Yes he was disappointed, but he also realised that he was very lucky to have her along at all; it was a miracle Patsy let her out. After just 6 lessons Megan finally found her confidence in the water and started to swim, gaining her NSA bronze award very quickly.

After 3 months of swimming club Megan asked Dr Williamson if little Trixie could come along, as she was also having an equally bad time at home with Patsy her mother, and she pointed out to him that she was terrified of water, and couldn't swim. He said yes immediately, and Trixie much to her joy and amazement started going along to the club every other Tuesday with Megan. She suddenly understood why Megan so loved the swimming club, making friends with all the other children, and why she was so fond of Dr Williamson, who treated them all like royalty. She realised that all the children felt his love for them pouring out of him as he walked the side of the pool, attended to their needs and fed them all before taking everyone home. They all felt so safe and loved when they were with him. It became a special time enjoyed by all, and for some it felt like the happiest time of their lives so far.

Dr Williamson always prayed and sometimes shed a tear when delivering these special little children back to their families, especially those that went home to a beating or a cold, unloving and lonely house.

Ten troublesome, almost drowning swimming lessons later, Trixie finally managed to master the water, much to the relief of all the instructors. She was one of the worst students they had ever had to teach, and at one point, nearly gave up on her, telling Dr Williamson not to bother bringing her again, as she would never swim, so bad was her fear of the water. He was absolutely furious, and flew into a rage, something that no one that knew him had ever seen before. He decided to take them all down a peg or two, refusing to give up on her, telling them that her confidence was in shreds and that if they came from a family like hers and Megan's, they too would struggle to achieve anything at all. He then pointed out that anyway, he paid for the pool and their tuition from his late wife's inheritance, so they could just bloody well get on with it, or sod off, and he would hire someone else. Needless to say they carried on, and eventually, Trixie managed to learn to swim.

Both girls loved their swimming club lessons and after 6 long months, it became their highlight. Trixie was getting so good to the amazement of the instructors, that she was actually now training for her NSA bronze award. Megan was developing fast in the water, and was training for her gold. Those nights were an escape for the both of them and helped to build their confidence. They always got home exhausted and slept better, much to the annoyance of the demon, who was doing his best to be as nasty and as noisy as possible.

It was a warm September day, and both girls had rushed home from school excited about going to the club that night. They gobbled down their tea and toast as quickly as possible, and were rushing to get ready when they suddenly realised that their bags were not prepared. Patsy always got their bags ready when she was home, and they were going to the club. Patsy was in a foul mood, and acting very agitated, though that was not unusual and she was already fuelled with sherry. Their brothers were sleeping over at a friend's house that night.

"Mum where's our stuff?" asked a worried looking Trixie.

"You won't need it tonight, he's not coming," she replied venomously.

"What?" screamed the two girls in unison. "He always comes at 6.30," replied a now tearful Trixie, not wanting to miss her swimming lesson.

Megan looked at her mother, her eyes glowing green, staring back at them in silence, a grin forming on her mouth, almost sneering at them.

"I'll get the bags," said Megan.

Trixie didn't understand why he wasn't coming to pick them up. He always came, he promised them all that he would always have their best interests at heart, and would always, until they were 18 of course, always, look after them, always!

Patsy's hackles were now raised. "He's not coming," she growled at them again, turning to sit back into her comfy chair and sipping sherry from her cup.

Megan knew something was amiss; their mother always knew when there was trouble, she sensed it, it was in the air. She also sensed it, but couldn't work out exactly what it was, so she went back upstairs and called out to Michael to come, and help explain this terrible vexing and nasty aura that was hanging in the house. It was making everyone very edgy, and she hoped that he'd be able to explain what had happened whilst she put the two swimming bags together. While she did this she told Trixie to remain downstairs.

The house remained quiet, no angels came, and the atmosphere started to change, evil seeping in through the walls, making it a nasty and really unpleasant place to be at that moment in time.

Megan and Trixie did what they usually did, and with their bags packed they sat on the arms of the sofa looking out of the living room window, waiting for the little white caravanette to appear, with Dr Williamson at the wheel, ready to take them to the pool. Six thirty came and went. Trixie was distraught, and still in tears. Their mother was sat in the kitchen in her comfy chair. The two girls took themselves to bed, cuddling in together to help ease the pain of their disappointment, praying under the sheets and giving thanks as the angel Michael suddenly appeared to stand guard over them in the corner of their little room, a very large sword firmly held in his hands.

Two very long days later, it was announced in the local Evening Post that Dr Darrell Williamson had been found dead at his house in Whitchurch slumped over his desk. He was actually sat making out the cheques that needed to be paid for the swimming pool and the instructors, and the gym; this was a regular routine payment he always made monthly.

He was only found after worried staff reported that he had not turned up for his clinics that day and was not answering his telephone, much to the distress of the patients who had been waiting for him to arrive, some for hours.

The police responded telling them that they could not do anything for 24 hours, and when pressed by the clinic staff the next day, the police finally agreed to visit his house, and saw him, through his office window, slumped over his desk. A doctor and an ambulance were immediately called, but after breaking down the door, he was pronounced dead at the scene. He had succumbed to a massive heart attack. After all the years he had worked as a doctor, helping to support his patients, he had actually died alone, with no one there to hold his hand or reassure him or even call an ambulance, like he had done hundreds of times as a doctor.

He died the way he lived, a lonely man, who dedicated his whole life to being the best doctor he could possibly be. The only good thing was that his beloved Gwennie was waiting for him when he passed. The smile on his dead face baffled everyone when they viewed his crumpled body, everyone except Sally Smith that is. When she saw him laid out in the morgue that same day as she was delivering the body of another person who had sadly died on her ward during her shift in Keynsham Hospital, she nodded and smiled. At least she would be able to tell the girls he wasn't alone when he died, well not in that sense anyway.

The outpouring of grief for the loss of this very special man was unbelievable. Older patients and children in their hundreds filled the church, and stood outside taking up every available space. The very distant relatives who were the only people left in his family had made the long trip down from Edinburgh for his funeral. They were totally shocked on seeing the masses of people who had turned up to pay their respects, not realising until his death what a special and very much loved man he was. They suddenly felt extremely proud that he was a very important, albeit distant, part of their family.

Megan and Trixie also felt his loss. Patsy was relieved. There would be no more interference in her life now, and she could once again relax, well for the moment anyway. Things for Megan and Trixie very quickly returned to normal: the baby still cried at night, something howled and scratched outside their window, and the door handle rattled every night, harder now than ever!

And so it was heads down back under the blankets, as situation normal had returned - well for now anyway.

Chapter 7

Elaine

Megan had met Elaine for the first time when Sally took her to the spiritualist's church for a Friday service and circle. Forty, single and broken hearted so many times, it was at this point of her life that she had given up on men. She was born to a lovely couple who were very devout and consequently was brought up strict Church of England. Her parents immediately put her into a Church of England school, to follow the ways of the Lord, and to learn how to be the best person you could possibly be without running astray, and trying the best you could to love and forgive anyone and everyone.

In her younger years, she had soon realised that she was very different to the children who went to school with her. She never really gelled with any of them and didn't really make friends. They all seemed so false, not genuine like her, and it was around the age of 9 that one day she suddenly heard someone talking to her inside her head. Thinking she was going mad, she decided to ask her mother about it that evening when she had come home from a very boring day at school. Her mother was in the kitchen reading a paper, while the evening meal bubbled on top of the stove. The conversation went like this.

"Mum, I'm going mad."

"Hello, darling, why are you going mad? Did you have a good day at school?" her mother asked with her head still buried in the local paper.

"There's a man talking to me in my head, and he won't go away. I have asked him to, but he keeps telling me he is my guide."

Her teary eyed mother jumped 3 feet up in the air, threw down the local rag and grabbed and kissed her daughter with sheer pride.

"Oh, my God, it's come!" she cried out.

"What's come?" a very confused Elaine asked.

"Your psychic gift of course."

"Mother you are frightening me, what do you mean?"

"Right let's sit down," suggested her mother.

They both grabbed a mug of tea and sat at the dinner table in the kitchen face to face, and emerged 3 hours later.

"Where's tea?" said her tired and grisly husband called Brian, coming through the kitchen door.

"It will be late tonight," said Elaine's mum who was called Jennifer.

"I've got skittles," he screeched back at her.

"Our Elaine has come to life."

"Oh sodding hell, more bloody ghost trouble. I'm pissed off with bloody ooky spooky."

"Sod off, you prat," Jennifer screamed back. "Get your own bloody tea elsewhere."

"I'll bloody do that," he said throwing down his work bag in the kitchen and stomping back out, not even bothering to change out of his work clothes.

"Silly bugger," said Jennifer.

"Oh, Mum, I'm sorry."

"Don't be," she replied. "We both knew that this time would come. He's so bloody selfish, he thinks of no one else but himself. Sod him, we have to get you sorted now," she said smiling. "Welcome to our world." She cuddled Elaine and shed a tear. *Oh well, here we go,* she thought.

Her mother was a very well-known Psychic Medium, but had always kept it very quiet within her neighbourhood. Her husband didn't believe in any of it and thought it all rubbish. "Bloody stuff and nonsense," he would always say. She never really talked about it to anyone, and at times it reduced her to tears. She chose to work away from home where nobody knew her. This suited her fine and she would travel all over the country, speaking on stage, and doing individual readings for people, including those that had to be kept a secret.

When her daughter was born, she realised that she would have a greater strength than she had ever had. When her gift emerged, and it would, she would encourage her to grab it and bloody well use it, not like her who probably only used about 20% of it, bowing down to an overbearing twit of a husband, who she married quickly, just to get away from her family. He was always dominant, never allowing her to use her gift around him or the family, never allowing her to mix with friends, or anyone like her at all, so her life of frustration was relieved every so often by going away for a few days to work with her angels, and come back home and slip into normal life as if nothing had happened at all. She never talked about it, and felt totally frustrated and unhappy, as everything always revolved around him. She would make damn sure her Elaine would never have to live like she did.

Over the next 20 years, Elaine followed her mother to every spiritual church meeting and gathering, much to the disgust of her father, who now rarely spoke to or even acknowledged her. She absorbed and learned everything she could, and at the age of 30 she could now stand on the lectern at the end of a spiritual church meeting, and pass on messages from the deceased to the public gathering, waiting in earnest to hear from their loved ones, which she did with almost 100% accuracy. She was good, really good, so good in fact that she was asked to do a tour. Television companies had even sent people to have readings and to listen to her messages at the end of the church meetings. They were ready to put her into the public eye, and let them see how good she was. They wanted her, and really good money was laid on the table, all she had to do was sign on the dotted line, but she refused. She was now at the top of her game, and getting 110% results, but she just felt she didn't have the confidence to go and do it because of love. The boyfriends came and went. They were all either smokers, drinkers, eccentric buggers or druggies, and no one really floated her boat. She was never really happy, and in fact she was miserable most of the time, and was still working at the council where she had been since she had left school.

Noisy neighbours, litter, damp and maintenance, her job was working with the public, a constant regime of complaints from the council tenants, and at times it bloody annoyed her, but she also loved it. She liked to get to know most of the tenants in her area and always tried to help as many as possible, because of course she could always pick out the genuine ones and the piss takers. Yes, this was her job, and she was good at it, and along with the church, she made it her life, and she loved it, and wouldn't change it for anyone or anything.

Chapter 8

Trouble In The Air

It would soon be bonfire night, time to start thinking about gathering wood, and asking neighbours for a donation of anything to burn on the eagerly anticipated bonfire. The neighbours along the street would always smile and hand over rubbish as they thought *"that will save me a trip to the tip"*, and so with a couple of weeks to go, Megan and her siblings, along with many other children who lived in the street, formed gangs that would work together to gather the much needed wood and items to burn.

Mr Rogers, was an old man who lived on his own in the ground floor flat just down the road from the Murphy family. He was in his late 80's, a widower and quite disabled from his World War I injuries, and the only contact with the outside world, was when he would go shopping once a week at the local shopping centre, and it was here he first met Megan. She always noticed him struggling with his bags, even though most of the times she was struggling herself, would always offer to help, and the given penny always refused, only to be pressed in her hand with a smile of gratitude from the old boy.

Megan now regularly visited and cooked for Mr Rogers once a week after school, normally on a Thursday but sometimes on a Friday, depending on her mother's working shift patterns. She would often amaze him by baking soda bread, beef stew and a corned beef hash on the same night, all of which were his favourites. He had a small fridge and chest freezer, so she could make a batch that would last him the week, and this he was always so grateful for, it made his life so much easier.

Today was Thursday, Megan had got home from school as normal, and her mother was already at home making the evening meal, pressing uniforms and clothes for the next day. She had worked a 6am to 3pm shift, leaving the house an early 5am in the morning, leaving Megan to get up, bake bread, and do all the usual chores, making beds and feeding her siblings before getting them all

45

off to school. It meant that when she came home on a Thursday and a Friday, she actually had some time to herself.

"Off to see Mr Rogers now," Megan said to her mother. The green eyed glare she received from her mother would normally knock another person off their feet, but Megan was used to it.

"What are you cooking him today?" she asked.

"I don't know," Megan replied, "depends on what he has got in the fridge, anyway, I was going to ask him for something for the bonfire."

"Well don't be late for tea! 6 o'clock."

"Ok," Megan replied skipping out of the door, through the back alley and out onto the road to make her way to Mr Rogers house.

When she arrived, she knocked twice - stopped, then knocked three times.

"Ok coming!" called out Mr Rogers. This was their signal to each other, he rarely opened the door to anyone these days unless he knew who they were, and had an appointment, trusting nobody.

Just as he was opening the door "Hello, Megan," called a little voice from behind her, it was Stuart Green, "can you give the old boy his paper for me?"

"Yes of course," she replied, as he passed over the weekly post to her. "Haven't seen you for a while, everything ok?" she asked him.

"Yes fine, but me gran's not been too good, so I have been helping out with Shelly."

"Oh sorry to hear gran's not good, are you coming to the bonfire party on bonfire night?"

"You bet I am. I will bring Shelly, you cooking?"

"Well, me and mum, jacket potatoes, hot dogs, soup and chilli, bring some pop and butter for the potatoes," she replied.

"Whoooo! Will do, I'll ask mum to come as well, she'll love that, what time?"

"Bonfire lights at 6, I will be there before to set up, fireworks around 7.30, eat at 8 okay?"

"Great," said Stuart, "see you there." He winked at Megan, smiling as he peddled away down the road. Megan smiled to herself, she liked Stuart.

"Come in, come in," called Mr Rogers.

"What are we cooking today?" she asked him.

"Well, I have some fresh chicken, veg, and garlic."

"Ohhhh," said Megan, "I love garlic, did you get any olive oil ?" she asked.

"Yes," said Mr Rogers, "two bottles."

"Great," she replied, "what are you fancying?"

"I bought some curry powder, do you know how to make a curry?"

She laughed. "Yes of course I do. Do you have any rice?"

"No, no oh bother I forgot that."

"Right," she replied. "I will get the curry cooking, it will take an hour or so, to get it nice and tender, and I will pop down the shops and get you some rice."

"Oh, love, you don't have to," he said.

"No worries, and while I am down the shops, you have a look for anything I can have for the bonfire?" she asked.

"Deal," he replied.

She quickly assembled the tasty curry, and placed it in a cast iron enamel roaster, popped the lid on and placed it in the hot pre lit oven. *That will need at least two slow hours*, she thought, opening the front door to go to the shops.

"Won't be long" she called out closing the door behind her.

Mr Rodgers was sat in his front room listening to the Dales on Radio Two, which would be followed by the Archers on Radio 4, whilst studying the crossword in the Guardian newspaper, leaving the weekly post on the sideboard, which he always read the very next day in the morning.

She ran down the road with a small shopping bag Mr Rodgers had bought for her begrudgingly, her mind was a whirl. Down the road, past the pub she ran, she was heading for the grocers which was next to the paper shop and the fish and chip shop.

She reached Jennings grocery shop and entered like a whirlwind, the shop was set out in two levels, a till at the entrance along the big plate glass window, which would allow the person at the till to see everyone who came in and out of the shop. The lower floor was a large square, with all the tins and packets, mostly placed along the back wall, bread and biscuits were on the middle isle, with all the household cleaners and washing powders etc along the wall as you entered. Upstairs on the next level was all the fresh fruit and veg, and a very large long fridge which contained all the blocks of cheeses which were cut by hand, butter, milk and cold meats, including sliced home cooked ham, black pudding, and rashers of bacon, which were lovingly prepared and cut on Albert's massive slicing machine, on the back shelf, so sharp, it could take your finger off before you knew it.

"Hi, Megan, how are you today?" called out Jenny.

"Fine," she replied, as she was scanning the rows of cans and packets. "Long grain rice?" she asked.

"Top shelf at the back next to the tins of Ambrosia rice pudding," Jenny replied, whilst she finished serving a young lad, without even looking up. Every position of every packet and tin, was ingrained in her brain, she always knew exactly where everything was placed.

"Cooking for mum?" she asked politely, when Megan came to the counter with the packet of rice, and her shopping bag.

"No, Mr Rodgers."

"What are you making?" Jenny asked.

"Chicken curry, and he wants rice," she replied, looking up to the ceiling.

"That will be lovely, you will have to make some for us sometime," she smiled back at her.

"One shilling please," said Jenny to Megan holding her hand out.

"Can I have a receipt please?" asked Megan politely, she always like to produce a receipt if she has been shopping for someone.

"Thank you, Mrs Jennings," she said putting the rice and receipt in the bag.

She ran out of the shop, not looking where she was going, and bumped straight into Stuart Green again.

"Slow down, whooa!!!" he called to her, laughing as he nearly fell over.

"Sorry," she cried with delight.

"Fancy seeing you again," he said, smiling at her as he chewed a jelly worm, which was hanging out of the side of his mouth, nearly choking on it.

"Mr Rodgers wanted curry tonight, but he forgot the rice, so I've had to come down and get it for him."

"Lucky, Mr Rodgers," he replied smiling.

"Stuart, are you ok? You look really tired." She looked at him and smiled.

"Oh, it's nothing really, I just can't seem to sleep at the moment, I'm hearing a bloody dog, or at least I think it's a dog, crying every night, I've even been out looking for it. I'll bloody kick its ass, if I find it, the other night I went out looking, it was almost as though it was right in front of me, it's 3 in the morning mind you, freezing cold, and I am in my pyjamas, looking for a bloody dog. It got scared when I shouted at it to shut up and get lost, then suddenly a bloody huge pair of yellow eyes appeared, and gave me the jumps it did, so I legged it back to the house. Could be a wolf you know, but I didn't hang around to find out, it's all I need with gran feeling unwell."

"Oh, God, he's a sensitive, and a good one," she thought before saying directly to him, "Stuart, please be careful, you just don't know what's around at night." Noticing the dark circles starting to appear under his eyes.

"Don't worry about me, gal," he said nicely, winking at her at the same time, making Megan blush, she felt her cheeks redden. "If I had a gun, I would shoot the bugger," he laughed. "Sweet?" he asked her, holding out the paper bag bulging with penny sweets. "I only usually have sweets on a Monday when I get paid, but I found a sixpence on my round tonight, can't keep much food down at the moment, but sweets seem to be ok, want one?" he again asked pushing the bag nearer.

"Megan, would you like to come to the pictures with me?" he asked with a gulp his neck reddening, it almost sounded like a guilty question, he was looking down at his shoes now.

"Love to!" Megan exclaimed with delight, without even thinking about it, then suddenly realising that her mother would never allow her to go out with a boy, especially at night, *"something is not right here with, Stuart,"* she thought, looking at his lovely smiling face, with his ginger hair, and freckles.

"Gotta go, babe."

"Go where?" she asked.

"Oh, all my mates meet every week up at the old guards hut to see the ghosts."

"What ghosts?" she replied shakily.

"Don't know, I've never seen anything, but apparently they are there." He laughed and, picking up his bike, started to make his way across the road to the muddy path, which lead up to the railway embankment, to the old guards hut.

"Be careful, Stuart!!" she cried out after him.

"Oh, God, Mr Rodgers, oh crap!!!" she cried out to herself. She quickly made her way up to the road, seeing Stuart disappear into the distance, and ran as fast as she could back to Mr Rodgers house.

She arrived red and puffing for breath. Mr Rodgers immediately opened the door, he had been looking out for her, worried something may have happened. *You never know in this day and age*, is what he would always say to himself.

"You ok, lass?" he asked, looking worried. "Why have you been so long."

"Sorry, Mr Rodgers, bumped into Stuart again, he's having some problems at home."

"Oh, poor bugger, sorry to hear that, he's a nice lad, nice family," he looked at her and winked.

"Right, let me see to the curry now," she said walking into the kitchen.

"Smells lovely, reminds me of the army," he said wistfully. "Always had a bloody good curry in the army," he again repeated with misty eyes.

"Well this one's going to be just as good," replied Megan, as she stirred the spicy mix, which made her feel very hungry herself now.

Megan cooked off two big servings of rice, and put two big rings of rice on two dinner plates, one for tonight, and one for tomorrow, adding two tablespoons of water in the centre of the rice which would produce steam, and heat the rice, whilst it was in the oven, covered with tin foil, this would keep the rice moist, and not let it dry out.

"There's another plate in the fridge for tomorrow," she called out as she opened the front door and let herself out, being careful to make sure the door was closed behind her. She ran as fast as she could back to her house, knowing she was late for her own tea.

She rushed in through the back door right into the angry glare of her mother.

"You're late," she growled at her.

"Sorry, Mum," Megan immediately replied to her looking down at her slightly muddy shoes and feeling a slight shudder down her spine, a swift clip came across her ear.

"Oh, Mum," she cried out.

"I told you not to be late."

"I know," screamed back Megan in sheer frustration. "There's trouble!" She somehow found the strength to yell at her, still not looking into the glowing green eyes.

"What trouble?" she asked aggressively, her eyes now giving away her agitation at the unfolding situation.

"It's Stuart, Stuart Green, a dogs howling, but it's not ours," Megan whispered back to her mother, blinking back tears.

"I know, I can hear it," her mother replied. She was deep in thought, once again a vicious sneer developed on her face making Megan instantly recoil.

"He's been out trying to find it, seen the eyes, not our eyes, big, massive yellow ones," she blurted back quietly, so as not to get any more attention from her brothers and sisters who were quietly chatting, whilst eating their tea.

"He's a sensitive, I think he's being drained." Her mother took her pinney off. "Your tea is in the oven, pudding is ready, eat yours, and dish up for them, I'll be back later." She put her coat on and quickly and quietly unnoticed by the other children left through the front door.

After the evening meal, with the house tidied and everything in order, everyone went to bed, but Megan laid awake, waiting to hear her mother return. The house was quiet, except for an odd dog like call, which could be heard in the distance. She got up out of bed, and went over to the window, slowly pulling back the curtains. No light was on in the room, so the outside view would be good. She could see nothing, but she could hear it, it made her shake, almost wobble, it was nasty, a terrible worrying feeling was creeping into her. She stood quietly looking out of the window listening to the call, her stomach gave a churn making her feel suddenly sick and clammy, the skin on the back of her neck was now rising, trouble was definitely out there, and where was her mother? Demons fed on fear, and this bugger wherever he was, was nasty, she was sure of it, her heart was now racing. She could feel the blood pumping through her veins, her head started to spin, he/it was near.

"He's feeding."

"Oh god, I hope it's not my mother he's feeding on. Angels help!" she called out, waking her sister.

"What's wrong?" Trixie called out to her, with her head under the covers.

"Nothing, Trix, don't worry,"

"Then get into bed," she cried in return.

Just out of the corner of her eye, Megan saw something, it blinked yellow, she took a deep breath, slammed the curtains closed, and jumped into bed, with such a force, the whole room shook.

Trixie started to scream out.

"It's ok, Trix, come in with me." Megan held the bedclothes open, and her little sister, within two seconds flat, was in at her side. "Angels please protect us!" Megan called out as they both pulled the blankets over their heads.

She heard the front door open and then close, she could hear her mother downstairs.

"Thank you," she called out to the angels in a whisper, and quickly fell asleep.

***

It was difficult for Megan to concentrate on her school lessons, what with the bonfire to think about, and Stuart, her mind was a whirl, and the atmosphere at school was quite odd. There was a hum, an anticipation of the forthcoming fireworks, bonfire and food that was firing their imagination for this special night. The history lesson which she normally loved was proving to be a problem, she was actually sat working out the ingredients for all the food she and her mother would be preparing. It was their job to provide all the cooked food that evening, and Megan's mother was a well- known cook and caterer, and nobody else in the street wanted to do it, so the families divided up between them the food, drink and fireworks, so it worked out fairer for all.

The Winter's Family were making hot punch, providing bottles of lemonade for the children, and beer and wine for the adults. The Dales and the Browns were providing the fireworks, and the Murphys the food. The list included jacket potatoes, chicken soup, chilli con carne, hot dogs with crispy fried onions, a real bonfire feast, which would be loved and devoured by all, and of course any remnants, would be fed to the family dogs back home.

She sat in the classroom totally engrossed with her list of food, suddenly noticing the dark clouds gathering outside. The rain started to fall, slowly at first, but then the fine rain turned into rivulets, emptying down as if a large plug had been suddenly taken out above.

"Oh, God," she thought, *"I'll have to walk the long way home tonight on the road, instead of crossing the horses field and up and across the train line."* She had already had a slap from her mother this week for muddy shoes and socks, and tonight was not a night for confrontation. The air was thick with trouble, Demon trouble brewing, and she was worried, no she would definitely go home via the main school gates and walk home as fast as possible.

The bell rang, Megan packed her beloved leather satchel with her books, lists and notes to look at before the next history lesson in a couple of days, and of course the lists of food needed that she knew her mother would ask her to provide for the bonfire food.

She made her way downstairs and along the corridor that would lead to the front school steps, and down past the tennis courts to the main school gate. When she reached the main gates the road was packed full of cars and parents waiting for their children, so she carefully threaded her way through the throng of gathering people at the entrance and started up the road. She was suddenly grabbed from behind, a pair of arms wrapping themselves around her and a big kiss planting on the side of her face. She nearly dropped to the ground with sudden fright, not expecting anything, just concentrating on making her way home. She was released, turned around, and there stood Sally Smith.

"Oh, God," cried Megan. "Sally, I've missed you so much."

"Not as much as I have missed you, Trixie and the boys, my darling."

Megan burst into tears, and Sally pulled her into her arms, and gave her a huge cuddle. "Oh, sweetheart, all of you haven't been out of my mind since the day they dragged you and Tinker away, are you okay?" she lovingly asked.

"Yes, yes, thank you," Megan stammered, hardly able to speak with emotion. "Trouble is coming," Megan blurted out through puffy teary red eyes.

"Yes, we know," replied Sally, and with that a horn sounded.

Megan and Sally looked over to the bright red Ford Escort with sporty wheels which was sounding the horn. "Hello!" shouted Claire and Elaine, who were waving furiously.

"Come on over, love," said Sally, pulling Megan by the hand to cross the road. "Get in, get in," said Sally. "We are taking you home tonight and don't want you getting in even more trouble for being soaking wet now do we?" Sally commented as the rain continued to pour down harder than ever.

"Thank you so much," said Megan getting into the back with Sally, "Claire, Elaine, how lovely to see you," cried a joyful Megan.

"You too, my darling," replied Claire and Elaine in unison.

"Mum knows," said Megan nervously.

"She bloody would," replied Claire.

"Now, now," intervened Sally. "Of course she would."

"It's not ours though," Megan blurted out.

"Are you sure?" asked Claire.

"Yes, I am now, he, it, was calling out last night, mine was quiet, definitely not the same. I have a nasty feeling."

"Yes, so do we," Elaine commented.

"Angels are gathering," said Claire. "Michael is very worried about you, well all of you actually."

"I know," replied Megan. "Animals are dying, terrible injuries, there was also some talk of the same kind of thing which happened about six months ago. It's been reported in the local post," said Megan.

"It's moving around feeding," replied Claire. "No wonder the angels are worried, and now it's moved onto our patch, animals won't be enough at some point, he needs a soul to feed on."

"There is a lad, a friend of mine he can hear it."

"WHAT!!!" exclaimed Claire, "WHERE?"

"Not far from us, down the end of the estate, he lives in a cul de sac, says he's been unable to sleep. He's seen the yellow eyes."

"Right, that's it," said Claire starting the engine. "Megan, we are taking you home, and if you don't mind a slight detour, show us where your friend lives. What's his name?" she asked her.

"Stuart," Megan replied, "Stuart Green."

"Well, Stuart Green, let' see if we can help you avoid being dog meat," Claire said.

"You mean demon meat," Elaine commented looking very worried at Megan and Sally sat in the back. Claire was now driving as fast as she could towards Megan's house, and the cul de sac.

All was quiet when they reached the cul de sac on the edge of the estate. They drove around and stopped to look at the view of the golf course. The rain was had become a slow drizzle and the golf course could be easily seen. What a view. It was truly breath taking, but an eerie sense was in the air, no birds flew around, no one could be seen, no dogs barked, really weird, silent and uncomfortable.

"He's not here!" said Claire.

"How do you know that?" asked Sally.

"He's not here, he's definitely somewhere else, he's just moving around here, stalking things out, I can feel a portal, it's not far away. I can sense it, it's within a mile. I can feel him, he's definitely not here."

"Why can Stuart hear him?" asked Megan.

"He's stalking him, he knows he's a sensitive," replied Claire. "Is he a sensitive?"

Claire turned and looked at Megan, "Yes," replied Megan. "A good one with a heart of gold."

"He's picked up Stuart's scent, and is stalking him, not good," said Claire.

"Bloody terrible if you ask me," Elaine cried out loud. "What are we going to do now?" she asked Claire.

"Well, first off, we are taking Megan home, and then we will have a little drive around to see if we can pick anything up."

"Can I come?" asked Megan nervously.

"No," said Sally. "Let's keep you on the right side of your mother, her senses will be heightened now, and she will be very agitated."

"Yes, she is," agreed Megan.

"Right then that settles it, home it is," Sally instructed Claire.

The engine started and they left the cul de sac, driving along the road towards Megan's house.

Just as Claire pulled up, Megan's front door opened, and her mother appeared on the doorstep, her eyes glowing green, angry and agitated she was looking directly at them all.

"Right, Megan, quick as you can get out," Sally pressed a small purse into Megan's hand. "This is for you. Two shillings to ring if you need me or you hear anything, anything at all. I have put my number inside the purse, okay love?"

"Okay, thanks," replied Megan as she got out of the car.

"Poor little cow," thought Claire. She could feel the glare of her mother, it would cut most people in half. Claire felt the holes burning into the side of her head, as she sat inside the car, she could feel the nasty and aggressive oppression that surrounded this house. She turned, smiled and waved at Megan's mother, all she got in return was a deep growl and a slight show of fangs.

"Oh, fuck me," exclaimed Elaine. "I wouldn't like to be in that house tonight."

Megan ran back to the car window. "Sorry, forgot to tell you, the old guard's hut on the train line down off of the main road, funny goings on being reported there, horses and cows dying in the field."

"That's it!" exclaimed an excited Claire. "That's the portal, his lair."

"Bye, Megan," called out all three in unison as the car pulled away at speed and roared off down the road.

"What did the witches want?" growled Megan's mother as she delivered a swift clip behind the ear.

"Oh, Mum, don't," Megan cried.

"What did they want?" she screamed louder this time.

"They know."

"What do they know?" again her mother asked.

"They know it's not ours. It's a rogue, a nasty one, a child and animal killer, they think he's after Stuart."

With that Megan's mother put her coat on, turned around and told Megan to get the tea. "It's all ready and keep everyone in, no playing out tonight, I'll be back later." She quickly slipped out of the front door.

Megan squeezed the little purse with the money Sally had given her in her hand and ran upstairs to hide it away safely, always worried that if her mother found it, she would take it and spend it on sherry.

A safe place underneath her dressing table was found, nice and secure and snug, she would only take it out, when it was needed, hiding it away from prying eyes.

That night was a quiet night, no child crying, no one going up and down the stairs, no growling or scratching at the window, nothing, sheer silence, eerie silence which worried her terribly. She heard her mother come in, all the children were in bed asleep, she hoped, but Megan could not sleep, her angels were also nowhere to be seen this especially worried her, trouble was definitely brewing.

"God help us all, " she prayed before nodding off to sleep.

Chapter 9

Fuel for the fire

The next day, Megan had a great day at school and was helping Mrs Evershott in the kitchen showing her how easy it was to make soda bread.

"Oh my!" she exclaimed to Megan. "That's beautiful, and so easy to make," she said as she bit into the warm wheaten bread smothered in butter. "Megan," she asked, "would you help me teach the class to make this?"

"Yes of course," Megan replied, feeling really happy inside.

"And I will help you get the best grades you can get in your CSE exams. Deal?" asked the teacher.

"Deal, thank you," said Megan.

Mrs Evershott squeezed Megan's hand. "Right then, soda bread it is, next week's lesson is sorted," she said smiling.

Megan rushed home from school, changed and before she left to go and cook for Mr Rogers, went to see her mother.

"Off to Mr Rogers?"

"Yes," replied Megan.

"Back by 6 and no messing," said her mother.

"Okay," she replied and made her way to the back door to go out through the alley before running down the road towards Mr Rogers' house.

When she arrived, a large council waggon was parked outside, and two men were taking the furniture out of one of the upstairs flats to be taken to the tip for disposal.

"Oh could we have that furniture for our bonfire please?" she asked in a puffed manner.

The two men stopped and looked at each other.

"That would save us a lot of bother," one of the council men replied.

"We could meet you after school at say 5 o'clock, and we will take everything you don't want to our bonfire and burn it on Guy Fawkes Night."

The two men looked at each other again.

"Okay, 5 o'clock it is then, lass."

"Thank you so much, I will go and tell everyone tonight, and we will be here at 5 o'clock tomorrow, thank you," she again repeated.

The two men went back up the stairs and closed the front door. "Don't worry, we will make sure that you will have the best bonfire around this year, all the furniture will burn, and you are also helping us, as we can now get on and get the other jobs we have lined up done. But don't let us down, and it will burn well." He winked at Megan.

"Thank you!" she called out again as Mr Rogers opened his front door hearing Megan conversing with the council men.

"Got a bargain there, girl," he smiled at her.

"What are we cooking tonight?" she asked smiling back as she walked into his flat.

"Lamb stew."

"Oh I love lamb stew, it's one of my favourites, but it won't be ready for about 2 hours, it needs time to tenderise," she explained.

"Oh that's okay," replied Mr Rogers, "I had a sandwich about 4 o'clock, I can wait. I have some lovely scrag end and a small breast of lamb that Darrell gave me."

"Oh that will melt, and be juicy and tasty," she replied as she set about making the heavenly stew.

All the lamb was floured with added salt and pepper before browning in a frying pan. The browned meat was then emptied into a large casserole dish, to which Megan added browned onion and garlic (Mr Rogers' favourite) chopped carrots, celery and parsnips. Next a couple of tins of chopped tomatoes, with chopped potatoes on top of them, fresh rosemary and thyme from the garden and a pint of water with 3 stock cubes crumbled in as well as the residue from the browning pan, were all added to make the flavour burst out. Then she mixed some butter and flour together to make a paste, just like her mother had taught her, and put the casserole on top of the stove bringing it gently up to boiling point, adding the paste so it melted into the mixture. It would then slowly thicken the whole stew as it was cooking. She had already knocked up a loaf of soda bread, which was just about to come out of the oven. The stew would go in when it came out, with just a tad more salt and pepper added to the casserole before she popped it in the oven. Job done!

"It's in!" she shouted to Mr Rogers. "It will be a good 2 maybe 2 and a half hours, but it will be lovely."

"Okay," he shouted back.

She went into the front room where he was sat listening to the Archers on the radio.

"Check it about 7.15, and give it a stir. The meat should be nice and tender and falling off the bone, if it's not, give it a bit longer," said Megan.

"Thank you," he replied and pushed a half crown into her hand.

"No really," she replied pushing his hand away.

"Yes really," demanded Mr Rogers. "I don't know what I would do without you coming here helping me, and you have brothers and a sister to look after as well, and a fucking bitch of a mother."

"No," cried Megan, "please you don't understand my mum, she's amazing, what she's been through, most people would have crumbled by now."

"Sorry, lass, I'm sorry, I didn't mean anything by it, but you know people talk."

"Yes, Mr Rogers I am aware but please tell people to shut up and ignore the gossip, my mum is wonderful."

Mr Rogers looked at her with a puzzled expression. "You sure?"

"Cross my heart," replied Megan giving him back the half crown. "See you tomorrow when we are collecting the furniture."

"I'll look forward to that," he replied.

"You need to come to the bonfire party," said Megan forcefully looking at him with a smile and a firm stare.

"I might just do that," he winked at her as she went to the door.

"Don't forget give the stew a stir so it thickens evenly."

"I will. Goodnight, young lady and once again, thank you."

She pulled the door closed behind her as she left him, and started to run down the road towards her house.

Five o'clock the next day could not come fast enough, and Megan along with her brothers and sister had managed to gather many of the gang members together to help with collecting the unwanted furniture which would help fuel the bonfire. They all walked down the road together in a long line, crossed over to Wallow Lane, then down along the back road to gather outside number 23, which was also Mr Rogers' flat. They were going to be taking the furniture from the top flat, and were there on the dot. Mr Rogers was busy making glasses of orange squash for the waiting children, when the two council workmen arrived in their open top lorry, which was always used for house clearances.

"My, we are keen," said the tall, unshaven, black haired workman as he got out of the lorry.

"What did I tell you, Kev," he said to the older workman, "keen as mustard to take all this old furniture for the bonfire. Makes our job easier," he laughed looking at the large group of children waiting at the bottom of the steps. "Right then, let's get this door open, and he quickly leaped up the steps 2 at a time until he reached the door to the flat. He took a key out of his pocket and opened up the treasure hole, which was exactly what it was for the children. "Come on, kids, but go steady now," he called. Everything was piled high in a heap in the middle of the front room floor. "We will take the cooker and the brass bed to the tip," Reg told them all, "everything else is burnable. Tell you what, me and Kev will go to the tip now with the bed and cooker, and be back at 7 o'clock, how does that sound? Whatever you have not taken, you can take the next day."

"Yes," shouted all the children.

"Hang on now, Kev and me will get all the heavy stuff down the stairs for you, and you can take it from there, okay?"

"Okay," they all called back, so Kev and Reg handled all the heavy furniture down the stairs and deposited it in Mr Rogers' front garden.

"Anything I can do to help?" he called to the two workmen.

"Nah, just keep an eye on these kids while we go to the tip, we don't want anyone falling down the stairs do we?" he laughed throwing a large chunk of brass bed into the lorry.

The children toiled for a whole hour, just carrying the old furniture across the field, down past the allotments to where their beloved and nicely swelling bonfire stood. They had virtually cleared the whole flat by the time most of them had to go home for their tea. It was a great feeling seeing the bonfire virtually double in size before their very eyes. They had taken everything, apart from one large armchair.

"Leave it," said Mr Rogers.

"Oh no, that will burn brilliantly," Megan replied. "Me, Trixie and Tinker will carry it."

"What about the lino?" asked Mr Rogers. "That will burn really well."

"Don't know if we have enough time tonight," Trixie called out.

"Well let's get this chair down and if we have enough time to come and get the lino we will, otherwise we will have to come back tomorrow," said Megan.

60

At that moment Kev and Reg returned from the tip. "Bloody hell, kids, that's amazing," said Kev.

"We would really like the lino because it will burn really well, but we are going to be called for our tea now, so we won't have time today," said Megan.

"Well what do you think, Reg?" said Kev, looking over to his mate.

Reg replied, "Since you kids have worked so hard, what about 5 o'clock tomorrow? But! You will literally have 20 minutes to get it out."

"Yeah!" cried the tired children as the flat door was pulled shut.

"Okay, see you all tomorrow at 5 o'clock," they called back to the kids as Kev and Reg got back into their lorry and drove away.

"Wonder if Mum will let us put this in the alley until Bonfire Night, so it doesn't get wet, and then it will burn really well," said Megan.

"Good idea," said Tinker. "Out the back under Dad's tarpaulin would be even better though, it would be out of the way there."

"That would work better," Trixie called out, so the three of them carried this precious chair which was really heavy, smelly and quite dirty and stained to their house. Goodness knows what the neighbours thought of this very funny sight, of three children wobbling down the road, with a huge armchair in their arms.

Chapter 10

A troubled mind

The chair was wedged next to the dog kennel outside the back door, with a tarpaulin placed securely over the top to keep the rain out. Megan's mother was cooking tea when they brought the chair home.

"Oh what crap have you brought home now?" she cried.

"Just an armchair for the bonfire," all three replied together.

"Why isn't it down the bonfire then?" she snarled back at them.

"It will get wet and not burn properly," Tinker replied.

"Right, well I want it gone Bonfire morning understood?"

"Okay!" all three replied looking at each other smiling and giggling at the same time.

Tea that night was a tender and succulent beef stew that Megan had helped her mother make the day before. Megan had come straight in from bringing that bloody chair into the back garden and made the herby dumplings. She gathered sage, chives, thyme and parsley from the garden and chopped them fine and put them all into a bowl. She then added self-raising flour, suet, salt, pepper and a teaspoon of baking powder, and mixed in the herbs, and a little water to make sticky dough. She then rolled them into little balls, before carefully placing them on top of the bubbling stew her mother had taken out of the oven, and placed it on top of the stove.

God, thought Megan, their eyes meeting and agreeing on the exact placement of each of the precious sticky balls that would swell, fluff and add amazing flavour to the stew,*I wish she would love me as much as I love her*.

"What are you staring at?" glared her mother almost embarrassed by her stare.

"Oh nothing," replied a shaky Megan.

"None of you are to go back out tonight understand?" she ordered.

"Oh, Mum I was going to the Collins' house tonight," wailed a distraught Tinker.

"No you are not," she bellowed. "Tonight everyone is early to bed. Now everyone to the front room until tea is ready," she ordered like a sergeant major.

They all trooped into the front room to settle in front of the little black and white television, and the roaring open fire. They watched Blue Peter, with their hungry bellies rumbling as they waited for their evening meal.

Megan's mother grabbed Megan's arm as she was passing and whispered quietly into her ear, "Keep an eye out and let me know if anything funny happens."

Megan silently nodded back to her, fear creeping into her thoughts now.

"Tea!" their mother called a little later on.

"Yeah!" they all cried back, as they rugby tackled each other out of the now warm and cosy front room, to go into the dining room to fill their hungry bellies.

The stew was delicious especially the dumplings, which were huge and fluffy. This was followed by rice pudding with a lovely thick crusty top, served with a dollop of homemade strawberry jam. It was heaven!

Sleep evaded Megan that night, as everything seemed wrong. The growling and scratching that she had always grown up with had stopped, and what she was hearing was something totally different. The atmosphere had changed, and the angel that always came in and out of her bedroom now had a sword.

That means trouble brewing, she thought.

Her head was constantly spinning thinking about the chair outside in the garden and wondering what was wrong with it. She decided that she would have another look at the chair the next day. Her thoughts were also on Stuart, and she decided to also try and see him and his family the next day and see how they all were.

The next morning Megan reminded everyone that they had to be at the flat for 5 o'clock to pick up the lino for the bonfire, then she ate her breakfast while washing-up the breakfast things. Before leaving the house with her brothers and sister, she had decided to stop in at the newsagents on the way to school and ask Mrs Drew if she could possibly pass on a message to Stuart.

"Yes of course, Megan," replied Mrs Drew.

"Please could you ask him to call in on our house?" said Megan.

"Will do," Mrs Drew replied.

"Thanks," Megan called as she skipped out of the shop on her way to school, with a small bag of cough candy twist which Mrs Drew had put into her satchel.

The day seemed to pass really slowly, and Megan found herself constantly thinking about that bloody chair in the backyard, and Stuart, not to mention Bonfire Night which was only 5 days away now. Once again she felt as if her head was spinning. Today was Friday and she had heard nothing from Stuart since she had bumped into him on Monday at the shop and at Mr Rogers' home. Her stomach churned, which was always a sign of problems to come, and still she was hearing this unusual calling. It was not her usual one, no definitely not, she was sure. But the growling, and scratching continued, not exactly outside, but now and again it would be up close, close enough to know someone or something was lurking and sniffing around outside.

Her angels had returned, and not only were they in her bedroom, but they were also walking around the house, which made her mother even nastier.

Oh, God what else? she thought as she walked home from school that day. Then she suddenly remembered that she had put the small brown purse Sally had given her in the bottom of her satchel that morning and decided that as soon as she saw a phone box she would call her.

Megan dialled the number and when the pips sounded pushed the A button and the penny into the slot.

"Hello, hello is that you, Sally?" Megan asked.

"Megan my darling, how are you? Thank you for calling; how's everything?" Sally enquired.

"I am really worried about my friend Stuart," said Megan.

"Right then, me girl," said Sally lovingly, "it's definitely a rogue demon, just as we thought. It's a nasty one, but as we have said, he is moving around, but is probably based at the old guard's hut. He is very well protected, and he is bringing in other spirits as well, though we don't really know how yet," said Sally.

"It's a portal," replied Megan.

"What!" exclaimed Sally.

"It's a portal, a gateway that opens into our world."

"How the bloody hell did you know?" Sally cried out in surprise.

"I think I've seen it, and it makes sense," said a now quite wobbly Megan, her stomach churning even more.

"God I must ring Claire, that's why we can't pin him down, he's coming in and out of our world, covering his tracks with all the other nasties, which he is using to distract us. Megan, I have got to go! I must ring Claire. Please keep in touch, darling. Love you!" she called out as she put the telephone down. Megan pushed the B button, and a halfpenny dropped out; the call had not been long enough to use the whole penny.

Great, thought Megan leaving the phone box and making her way home.

Chapter 11

Fish & chip night

Friday night was usually fish and chip night if it could be afforded, and thank goodness Megan's mother could afford it that night.

Megan was sent down to the chip shop with an order of 5 cod and chips. Patsy was making the mushy peas with the dried peas she had soaked overnight, boiling them up in salted water, then adding butter, salt and pepper and a splash of malt vinegar right at the end to tang them up. It would be served with freshly bought white sliced bread which was all the rage and very new, which would be spread thickly with creamy butter, just right for a chip butty, which the children loved so much.

"Call into the off license on the way home," she was instructed. "Give them this letter and wait."

"Okay," replied Megan. She then started to make her way down to the chip shop for the precious food they would be eating later.

It was about 6 o'clock when she approached the chip shop carrying her newly purchased shopping bag, which she would use to take the fish and chips home in, when she suddenly saw Stuart coming out of the newsagents.

"Stuart!" she called out to him. He saw her and began to make his way over to her. "Stuart, oh, God what's wrong?" He looked absolutely terrible and gaunt. His eyes were sunken, with black rings around them.

"Oh nothing, babe, don't worry about me. I'm just having a little problem sleeping that's all."

"Are you eating properly?" Megan asked him.

"All I can really eat is sweets," he replied.

Oh no, he's in trouble, bloody demon, she thought. His eyes were glazed and bloodshot.

"Got to go, Megan," he said as he started to make his way across the road.

"Where are you going?" she called out after him.

"Up to the old guard's hut," he replied pointing.

"Stuart please don't go there tonight!" she called after him.

He turned round and growled at her, his yellow eyes glaring.

Oh no, that's not him at all, she thought.

He carried on across the road, to make his way up the muddy path that led to the train line, and that bloody old guard's hut. That was the last time that Megan would ever see him alive.

Megan decided to turn around and go and ring Sally. She ran to the phone box but there were at least 6 other people waiting to make calls, and that would make her very late.

Oh no, she thought, *I can't be that late,* and ran back down to the chip shop noticing the funny aura coming from the area around the guard's hut.

"It's there," she said to herself.

"Hi, Megan," called Jenny Davis the assistant in the chip shop, "what will it be tonight?"

"Five cod and chips, thank you."

"Five cod and chips coming up. Bag of scrumps?" she asked her.

"Oh yes please, thank you," replied an excited and by now very hungry Megan.

"Salt and pickled onion vinegar on everyone's?"

"Yes, that would be great," Megan replied with a large smile on her face and she was soon making her way out of the shop with her precious load, and up towards the local pub, and the off license.

"That smells good," came a voice from behind the counter as she entered. "Hello, Megan.

How are you and the family and what can I do for you today?" asked the barman, Alan Lawrence.

She handed him the letter, which he opened and read, and a ten shilling note fell out.

"Okay, one moment." He returned a few moments later with a large bottle in a bag.

"The change is back in the envelope," he said handing her the bag and the envelope.

"Here, have a packet of crisps on me," he smiled as he handed her a packet of cheese and onion crisps. *Poor little cow*, he thought.

"Bye," Megan called and smiling back as she left the off license to go home. She was praying again; "Please, angels, look after Stuart before it's too late," but little did she know, it was already beginning to be too late!

Friday night's fish and chips were always thoroughly enjoyed by all, especially with the precious pickled onion vinegar reminding them all of Ireland. Megan really missed the little cottage, Granny, Jonny and her nieces and nephews who lived there, and she often said a prayer at night asking her angels to keep them all safe and most of all, not to let them forget her.

Their fish and chip meal, supplemented with mushy peas and bread and butter, left them all feeling satiated and full up to the gunnels and a pudding was never needed. They were also allowed a glass of cold Corona shandy which they all loved. As far as this little family were concerned, Friday night suppers just couldn't get any better.

"Oh, God!" Megan suddenly shouted out, while everyone was sat at the table. "We didn't go back for the lino." With everything going on, fetching the fish and chips, meeting Stuart and realising there was something wrong over at the guard's hut, she had totally and utterly forgotten to remind everyone about the lino at the flat. "Mum, can I run down and straight back to Mr Rogers'?" asked a now very flustered Megan.

"What for?" asked her mother.

"To see if the council men came today. If not I can leave a message with Mr Rogers and we can be there at 5 o'clock Monday for the lino."

"Tinker!" her mother called.

"Yes," said Tinker.

"Go with your sister down to Mr Rogers', but come straight back, and I mean run!" she growled.

"Thanks, Mum," cried Megan and Tinker as they both rushed out of the door.

As they were running down the street to the empty flat, Megan noticed they had company.

Angels were running either side of them.

God it must be bad, she thought as they ran down the road, and on arriving at Mr Rogers', she did her special knock on his door.

"Okay, okay!" called Mr Rogers as he made his way to the door. "Megan, Tinker what's the matter?" the old man asked looking at the two bewildered children puffing heavily on his doorstep.

"We forgot to come and get the lino," cried Tinker.

"Did the council men turn up today?" asked Megan.

"Well funny you should say that, they did, and left saying they were both going to retire, even left the door of the flat open when they left."

"Could we come and get the lino tomorrow, Mr Rogers?" asked Megan almost begging.

"Yes, of course," he replied, "they left me the keys. See you tomorrow afternoon, after you have finished shopping."

"Great, thank you," they both replied.

"Right then, both of you straight home, there's something nasty in the air tonight."

"Bye!" they both shouted and waved at him as they started running back down the road as fast as their little legs would take them.

Chapter 12

Exciting discovery

Saturday was a normal Saturday. Megan was up early with chores to do. There were beds to strip and remake, the bathroom and toilet to be cleaned, and then shopping, but today there was added pressure. On top of everything else, Megan was asked to go to the allotment and gather some veg with Mr Winters for Sunday's lunch.

Megan's mother had bought a very nice new shopping trolley on wheels, and had decided to accompany Megan on her shopping trip that day, which really agitated Megan as, she wouldn't be able to buy a blackcurrant ice cream, which was her little secret shopping treat and they would both have to walk the long way round up to the shopping centre via the road. It was already 3 o'clock and it would make her late picking up the lino.

She gulped down her lunch consisting of quiche Lorraine, salad and jacket potato, so fast that it burnt the inside of her mouth.

"Come on, come on," Megan said urging her brothers and sister to finish their meals as quickly as possible, because she wanted to get the washing-up done, so she could accompany her mother up to the shops, as soon as possible. It would soon be late afternoon, not a time in the day either of them wished to be out, especially now.

"Okay, Mum, let's go," said Megan once she had finished the washing-up.

They walked in silence, not a word spoken between them. Megan's mother never really spoke to her unless she had to. She never asked about school, or how she was, nothing like that, just barked orders at her, and today was no different. In a funny way, Megan had got used to it, and just accepted that this was the way it was, but deep in her mind, she made a promise to herself that if and when - no when - she had children, she would never, ever treat them the way she was treated. She would love them, cuddle them, play with them and be a great mum, not that her mum wasn't a great mum, she just didn't know how to show it.

They started the shopping, and as it was by now late afternoon and the usual thick crowds of shoppers had thinned considerably; just a few couples and a number of children were dotted around the usually packed shopping centre, making it easier to get around without queuing or bumping into anyone. It was *Fine Fare* first; all the heavy cans and packets going straight into the trolley.

Oh that will save my fingers, Megan thought. Then she was sent to the chemist to get toothpaste and the beloved Olive Oil, while her mother went to see Mr Brittain who owned the toy shop, to pay him, and sort out the Christmas toys.

When Megan returned, she found her mother waiting for her, sat on one of the long concrete benches outside the supermarket.

"Butchers next," she said.

"Okay," replied Megan. She took the list and the £10 note, and headed towards the butchers, with her mother walking a pace away behind her.

"Hello, Darren," called Megan.

"Hey, gorgeous girl, how are you?" Darren replied. "Hello is this Mum?" he asked in a very surprised manner. "What will it be today, girls?" he asked them smiling, finding it hard to keep his tongue in his mouth, and a large bulge from protruding in the front of his trousers!

Megan's mother was stunning. She was tall, with long blonde hair, a great figure, and long long legs, and the biggest green eyes you ever saw, and when she smiled she really was truly beautiful.

That's why I love my mum, Megan thought and within 10 seconds her mum had Darren eating out of her hands. The boys in the back of the shop were all sticking their heads out from the cutting room, whistling low wolf whistles, which of course she totally ignored. Megan just stood next to her mother, and watched them both conversing with each other and took it all in with pride, smiling as large bags of meat passed over the counter and a crisp £5 note was passed back.

God, Mum, how did you manage that? Megan once again asked herself. *That was 2 weeks' worth of meat, and all for £5.*

They left the shop with a very smitten Darren helping them out of the shop, down the little steps and loading the meat for them into their shopping trolley.

"Can't wait to see you again," he was saying to Megan's mother almost entranced.

"Thank you," Megan said and they made their way to Paulette's fruit and veg shop next door.

Megan's mother turned, her big eyes glowing bright green.

"You get the fruit and veg, I'll wait here," she ordered. The boys in the butchers shop and Darren were still ogling Megan's mother through the window.

"Hello, Megan," Paulette called from the back of the shop, "how are you today?"

"Fine thank you," she replied.

"God, who's that out there?" she asked.

"That's Mum," Megan replied.

"Wow, she looks good, I haven't seen her for a long time," Paulette said.

"She works really long hours," Megan replied.

Umm, I don't know why, but I have a funny feeling, I really don't like that lady, Paulette thought and instantly, as if she actually heard her thoughts, Megan's mother turned and looked directly at Paulette. *Oh, God, that's why.* Suddenly unnerved she served Megan as fast as she could. "I've popped a couple of large oranges, and apples in, on the house," said Paulette. "A thank you for being such a good customer."

Megan smiled and thanked her and then made her way out of the shop to join her mother for the long walk home.

"Come on now, be quick," Megan's mother shouted to her. The light was fading fast.

"I still have to go and get the lino when I get home," she commented to her mother.

"You will only go if your brothers are home, and they can go with you," she replied sharply.

"Oh goodness, I hope they are," Megan mumbled to herself quietly and thankfully they were.

Once the shopping was put away, Megan went upstairs and changed into her play clothes, but a chilling call she heard outside, made her stop in her tracks. Her heartbeat was harder and faster, and a tingle went flying down her spine and into her stomach, making her suddenly feel very sick and wobbly.

"Oh, Lord and angels," she called out loud. *I do hope Stuart's okay*, she suddenly thought.

The three of them ran down the road towards Mr Rogers' flat. The usual knock from Megan brought Mr Rogers to the door.

"Hello all of you, I'll just get the keys," he said to them very cheerily. "Now, let's let you all in," he added as he climbed the stairs up to the flat door.

The flat was totally trashed, and every bit of lino in every room was torn to shreds and piled up in the middle of each room.

"What's gone on here?" exclaimed Mr Rogers in shock. "What a mess. You won't be able to take any of this, kids. I'm sorry I'll have to ring the council back."

"What about this bit?" Megan asked walking to the corner of the front room where a large triangle of lino was still intact. "We could take this piece; it would help the bonfire burn."

"Okay, that'll be fine," he said. "I will see you downstairs when you have finished. Pull the door closed behind you," he said to them as he left.

Megan and her brothers had started pulling up the thin lino from the floor, when suddenly as they pulled £5 notes started floating up into the air.

"What the hell! Mr Rogers! Mr Rogers!" the children screamed out loud.

Poor Mr Rogers on hearing their cries got up the steps as quick as his crippled legs could take him. "I'm not a young man anymore," he called out coming up the stairs. "What the bloody hell?" he stated in sheer surprise at the sight in front of him.

Five pound notes were floating all around the room now, the harder they pulled up the lino the more that were being discovered. They had all been taped by selotape, which had long since perished releasing the bundles of hidden money for all to see.

"Oh no, oh no, now I understand what those two buggers meant by their comments on retiring. Oh, sorry, kids, gather it all up. I'll go next door to Irene, she has a telephone; we must call the police."

While Mr Rogers was next door calling the police, Megan told her younger brother to run down and tell their mum what had happened, and that they would be late for tea. Within 10 minutes flat it felt like a whirlwind had arrived, with sparks and flashes spraying all up in the air outside. Their mother had arrived at the flat.

"Kids out now!" she screamed at the top of her voice, making the walls shake.

Mr Rogers had just limped his way up the steps again. "Hello you must be Mum, I'm Mr Rogers."

"The kids' tea is ready and I want them home now," she barked at him.

"That's fine," said Mr Rogers, "the police are on their way. I reckon the old boy put all his savings under the lino. Sad really, he never had any visitors, only a daughter perhaps twice a year. That's why I am so grateful for Megan coming and helping me. Kev and Reg must have found it all; no wonder they told me they were retiring, the buggers. Let's just quickly count it all up so I can give it to the police."

They quickly counted the notes and found that it totalled £955. None of them had ever seen that amount of money before. It was all piled up in bundles in the middle of the bare floor, and everyone sat silently staring at this fortune they knew would never be theirs, and with that the police arrived.

Sergeant William Brown was the local Sargent, and well known In the area for his strict and uncompromising policing, He had gotten to know most of the local residents and kept a special eye on the good and bad ones, and especially troublesome families, and knew of most of the residents who lived on the surrounding estates as well, if there was anything, anything at all going on, he made it his business to know about it! In any way he could often paying for information using underhanded and secretive people to do his dirty work.

"Hello, everyone," he said as he walked into the flat, "what exactly is going on here?" he asked.

"Can I take the children for their tea?" Megan's mother asked. "Mr Rogers will fill you in. Here's the money the kids found tonight, and here's our address. We are the first house down the road next to the lane that leads to the allotments."

"Fine," replied the sergeant. Acknowledging Patsy and the children "Mr Rogers, what can you tell me about all of this?" he was asking as the family left.

"Oh, God what a nightmare," Megan said as they were walking back very briskly down the road towards their house. The night sky was worrying. Lights flashed around, and blues and greens swirled in the sky like cotton wool trails. "Something really bad is brewing," she cried.

Megan's mother looked back at her and screamed, "Quiet!" before pulling Trixie along even faster in an effort to make it home as quickly as possible. The two boys quietly jogged along right behind them.

Chapter 13

Reward

Sunday turned out to be a quietish day. They were having roast capon for dinner, a huge 6lb bird that would leave plenty of cold meat for Monday night's tea, cold chicken, homemade coleslaw and crispy cheese filled jacket potatoes. Oh and of course for the boys, Branston Pickle.

Most of the washing was finished the day before so it was ironing school uniforms and more housework today. Megan was asked to go down to the allotment, and see what Mr Winters had put to one side in the small shed on their patch.

Walking down through the muddy lane to the allotment gate, she could see the bonfire standing straight and tall just over the way, ready for the Guy Fawkes. This would be made from old clothes and sewn together and stuffed with old tights and socks and, anything combustible that would burn well. This would then be placed with pride at the very top of the bonfire, such was the tradition.

"Hey, Megan," called Mr Winters.

"Hello," she replied, "can I help you with anything?" she asked him.

"No all done now, sprouts, parsnips and carrots, and some potatoes and a few nice leeks," he said pointing to the mounds of vegetables lying on the ground covered in mud.

"Oh, wonderful, thank you," Megan replied starting to stuff the muddy veg into baskets.

"Here," said Mr Winters taking them, and dipping all the muddy veg into a large oval tin bath filled with rainwater, and swirling them all around, releasing the mud. A quick shake later and the baskets were quickly filled with clean vegetables. "Some bonfire this year," he said pointing to it.

"Yes it will be fab, biggest in the area," replied Megan.

"What are you cooking?" he asked.

"Jacket potatoes, hot dogs and fried onions, chicken soup and chilli."

"A veritable feast," he smiled. "I can't wait; your food is always wonderful. I wish my wife could cook like the two of you."

"Are Tony and Lilian coming?" Megan asked.

"Oh yes, don't worry, they have spent the week in Norfolk with their gran, but they will be home tonight."

"Great, are they making the Guy Fawkes?" she asked.

"Should they be?" asked a very concerned looking Mr Winters.

"Well, yes if you don't mind?" she replied. "It's the only job that's not allocated."

"Well then, consider it done. We will get onto it as soon as they are home."

"Thank you," replied an excited and smiling Megan.

"You are very welcome, young lady," he replied. "By the way, have you heard that bloody wolf crying at night? Oops, excuse the language."

"Wolf!" exclaimed Megan.

"Yes it sounds just like one."

"It's probably a stray dog, lost and crying for its owner," she replied nervously.

"It always seems to be at the back of our houses," he stated. "If I see it, it'll get the bloody pointed end of my boot right up its jaxxi! Noisy beggar."

"Must go, Mr Winters, got to help Mum with the dinner."

"Oh yes, Megan do go, see you again soon."

"Tuesday," Megan called back.

He waved. "With the Guy Fawkes," he shouted back.

Megan started with the stuffing, bashing stale breadcrumbs that she had saved all week, into fine crumbs before adding them into a mixing bowl along with chopped sage, thyme and parsley all fresh from the garden. A large white sweated down onion was also added. Two skinned pork sausages, a can of apricots finely chopped, with the juice, and one beaten egg were all mixed together with a little warm water, salt and pepper until a nice thick consistency was reached.

The cavity of the bird was seasoned, and the stuffing inserted along with half a lemon. Butter, and salt and pepper were smeared all over the bird, which was then wrapped with smoked streaky bacon and placed on a trivet over water to help steam. Whilst cooking, the bird was wrapped in silver foil, and placed to one side to come up to room temperature before being placed in the oven.

There was going to be parsnip mash, roasted carrots with fresh thyme and butter, cabbage, and wonderful leeks in creamy cheese sauce. Orange and thyme gravy would accompany duck fat (from Darren of course, one of his little specialities) and roast potatoes. It would be a feast, she decided while she helped her mother prepare everything under the watchful eye of the smiling blue lady standing in the corner, she had always appeared to Megan ever since she was born, and again today she stood in her usual corner in the kitchen just being there for Megan saying nothing looking on at the family scene and smiling, just like a guardian angel, which in turn made Patsy moody and evil. Not wanting the attention, making it difficult for her to keep her own demon under control.

"We are not burning the chair on the bonfire," said Megan's mother suddenly.

Megan stopped what she was doing and looked at her absolutely astonished. "Why not?" she asked.

"Because I like it, and God only knows we need a bit of comfort in this house. It's a very comfortable chair," she added.

"But it stinks and is filthy," Megan replied sternly.

"It's not now," Megan's mother retorted looking at her before looking back down into the cup of sherry she was fingering, clearly deep in thought.

Megan dropped her knife and ran outside, pulling back the tarpaulin. The chair gleamed, her mother must have spent hours scrubbing and cleaning it, as all the stains had gone and it didn't look half bad.

"Oh goodness, Mum, what a transformation!" she declared.

"I know it's a bit worn, but I will go and get some fabric next week and recover it. It'll do fine."

But there was something about that chair that Megan could not get out of her mind.

What on earth is it? she wondered, now feeling anxious and not knowing why this chair stood out in her mind so much.

Dinner was wonderful. The capon was juicy and delicious, the stuffing perfect, and the veg and gravy were to die for. It was almost a Christmas Day dinner, all the children readily agreed. Pudding was a light Birds trifle made for quickness, and it would be toasted cheese and pickle sandwiches for supper.

Sunday was always a lovely day. It was a day to indulge and relish the food that was made with so much love, and as always the highlight of this family's week. Everyone was stuffed now, and as she washed up the dishes Megan found herself wondering how any of them would be able to manage supper.

No one was allowed out to play as it was now getting darker in the early evening, and anyway, homework had to be done. School uniforms were already hung up on the line ready for the next day, and Sunday night was bath night, then television for an hour, watching mother's favourite programme, the Black and White Minstrel show, supper and bed.

They had all gathered in the tiny front room in front of a roaring fire, and were all bathed and in their PJ's, when there was a knock at the front door. It was Sergeant William Brown and his sidekick, PC Flower.

"May we come in?" the sergeant asked as Megan opened the front door. Her mother quickly and suddenly appeared at her side, as if by magic.

"Yes of course," Patsy replied. "What can I do for you, Sergeant?"

"Sorry to call on a Sunday, but I have come straight from the daughter of the deceased gentleman whose money you found in the flat yesterday, and kindly reported to us. The two council workers have been arrested and charged with theft. They had over £3,000 of the old boy's money in their possession, and along with the £955 you found, all of it has been returned to his daughter." In his hand he held a brown envelope. "She wanted you to have this, and said thank you for your honesty."

"We don't want it," replied Megan's mother tartly, "we don't take charity. This house works for its money."

"Mummy!" cried out all 4 children at the same time.

"It's not charity," replied Sergeant Brown, looking straight into those alluring green glowing eyes, "think of it as a reward for your honesty. If you hadn't reported it, those beggars would have got away with a fortune. Now please take it, give it to the kids if you must, but please take it; she wants you to have it."

Sergeant Brown looked around the sparse but incredibly clean house as Megan's mother took the envelope.

God these kids could do with some comfort, he thought.

When Megan's mother opened the envelope she found that there was £50 inside.

"There you go, that could be a little holiday for you all in Weymouth for a week," said the sergeant.

The children all screamed with delight. They had often gone to Ireland to their granny's cottage, but that wasn't a real holiday, because they all had to work while they were there. The nearest they had ever gotten to a holiday was when their mother had enough money to take them all on the train to Weston-Super-Mare. Now that was a real adventure, and a great treat.

Megan's mother looked at Sergeant Brown and said nothing.

"Right then, we'll say goodnight to you all." He tipped his hat and pushed PC Flower out of the door into the cooling night air. Once outside Sergeant Brown exclaimed, "God, what was it all about in there? The atmosphere in that bloody house gave me the willies."

"Oh, I'd love to give her the willy," PC Flower blurted out. "Sassy looking lass that. Oh I could imagine my hands all over her."

"Edmund!" screamed Sergeant Brown. "Keep your bloody lurid thoughts to yourself while we are on duty." Inside the sergeant was thinking exactly the same thing. *She's a bloody witch that's what she is*, he decided inwardly. *Put a bloody spell on us both.*

How right he was!

It was a demon thing. *Oh human men are so easy to wind up*, Megan's mother thought smiling as she was making the toasted sandwiches for supper that evening.

Chapter 14

Stuart Green

It was the day before Bonfire Night, and Stuart had come home from school as normal, quickly got changed, grabbed his bike from the shed, and then said goodbye to Shelly his little sister, and then his gran.

"Don't be late for tea at 6 o'clock," his gran had called out after him.

"Okay, I won't," he shouted back as he frantically pedaled down the path on his way to collect the papers for his round.

Being Monday it was also payday, always a good day. He always treated himself and Shelly to a bag of pick 'n' mix, which he took home after finishing his round, and handed them over with pride.

Shirley and David Drew were in their late 60's and almost ready to retire from their newsagents shop. For 40 years they had lovingly served their customers, toiling night and day 7 days a week, and getting up every day at 4am to wait for the arriving newspapers and magazines which their regular and grateful customers totally relied upon. Every morning the shop would open at 5.30am to catch the early workers that would be making their way to the local bus stop right opposite the shop, for their journey into the city. The first bus would arrive at 5.45am and would always be full. Early morning business was brisk, and very fruitful, Shirley making up sandwiches and rolls to sell to the sleepy morning crowds, all of which added to the takings, and their retirement fund.

An evening paper would then arrive about 3.30pm ready to be delivered by the local paperboy or girl so customers could catch up with all the local and nationwide news that they had missed while at work during the day.

"Hello, Stuart, had a good day at school?" Shirley Drew asked him as he fell through the door cheeks all ruddy and puffing from riding his bike at breakneck speed to the shop.

"Yes thank you. How many tonight?" he asked.

"Busy tonight, my darling," she replied not looking up at him while she filled his large bright fluorescent green paper bag, "Twenty-three Evening Posts and 10 late green uns. I'll have your wages ready for when you get back. Two bags of pick 'n' mix as well?" she asked him smiling.

Stuart turned and smiled. "Thanks," he said before popping the 2 bright green heavy laden paper delivery bags over his shoulder and leaving the shop.

"Nice lad that," said Mr Drew, "never lets us down. Give him the sweets tonight, love, he's always on time. Can't say the same for those other lazy beggars."

Mrs Drew smiled at her husband. "I'll put a couple of extra flying saucers in, Shelly will love them," she said and filled two paper bags with a mix of penny sweets and put them on the side for when Stuart came back, along with 5 shillings, which was his weekly pay.

One shilling a day for 2 rounds x 5 days = 5 shillings. They paid the best rates around, because they believed if they paid the best, they would get the best, and Stuart never, ever disappointed them.

Fifty minutes later he was back, his cheeks still ruddy and puffed.

"Okay?" asked Mrs Drew.

"Fine, no problems," he replied. "Mrs Marsh of Turner Street, not my round," he stuttered, "her Sun was wet and damaged yesterday."

"Oh, God not again," mumbled Mr Drew. "That'll be Nancy. She never likes their dog as it always tries to bite her she says, so she leaves the paper on the doorstep. No wonder it gets soaked. I will have to have a word," he said. "There you go, Stuart, your wages and the sweets are on us this week. Oh and remind your mum, 2 weeks left to pay on the Christmas club," he said with a smile and a wink. "You're looking tired, me lad," he added.

"Yes, trouble sleeping at night. There's a flipping dog, growling and barking all night. I have tried to find out who it belongs to, but no luck though. Could I leave my bike chained up outside until I come back later? I am meeting up with friends at the deserted guard's hut on the railway."

"Yes of course, love, mind no one pinches it though," said Mrs Drew.

"Nah, I'll chain it up good and proper. See ya," he said heading outside, to run across the road, before heading up over the muddy track and towards the deserted guard's hut up on the old train line.

Chapter 15

The surprise

That same day, Megan had got home from school as fast as her legs would take her. Tea that night was the cold chicken, and bubble and squeak to use up the leftover cabbage, carrots and cheesy leeks.

"This will be wonderful," she quietly said to herself in the kitchen, looking inside the fridge, which was bursting with cooked veg.

She ran upstairs to change, and was carefully putting her school clothes in a neat pile on the bottom of the bed for pressing later, along with all the other school clothes, when she noticed a note addressed to her on her pillow.

The note read:

Dear Megan, please be careful wherever you go now. Whatever you do, stay in if possible at night and keep your brothers and sister in as well. You will all be safe tomorrow, we will be watching. Have a lovely Bonfire Night; we know how much it means to you all. Keep in touch, and phone me Wednesday.

We all love you, special girl.

Signed Sally, Claire and Elaine.

This made Megan shake. *Something really bad is about to happen, I'm sure*, she thought and with that Michael suddenly appeared in the corner of the bedroom, with a very large and rather sharp looking sword.

"Don't worry, child we are here," he said then disappeared.

"Christ you had better be please!" she called out loud into the room.

"What's up?" Trixie asked coming to the top of the stairs.

"Oh nothing, just me being silly again," she replied. "Hungry?"

"Starving," came Trixie's very quick reply.

"Good, tea will be about an hour, go and make yourself some toast and Marmite. Jam's all gone until shopping. Are the boys back?" Megan asked.

"Just coming in now," replied Trixie.

"Right go on then, it's your turn, I'll start cooking tea, and don't make a mess!" she said leaving the bedroom.

The cold chicken was already dissected and sliced on a plate in the fridge and covered with foil.

Megan chopped and sweated an onion, then chopped the cold roast potatoes, parsnip mash, carrots and cabbage and mixed it all together, and then added the cooked onions, salt, pepper and a large knob of butter. She then buttered a baking dish, and piled all the mixture in, dotting the top with little dollops of butter and the last of the leftover grated cheese from the sandwiches the night before. It was then all drizzled with a little olive oil, and some fresh thyme from the garden. Job done.

She would leave it in the oven on a low temperature for about an hour, turning the heat up in the last 15 minutes to crisp up the top.

"Oh sod it!" she exclaimed. "No Branston Pickle. The boys won't eat it without it."

The jar was empty. The boys would go mad and refuse to eat the bubble and squeak without the godly pickle they so loved.

There was a note from her mum and a ten shilling note on the dresser with orders for Megan to go to the off license for her usual.

Oh no, thought Megan remembering the note she found on her pillow. "Bugger, I'll have to run like mad," she said to herself. "Kids!" she called as she entered the front room to the sight of 3 kids munching on toast and Marmite and drinking hot tea. "Right, I've got to go to the shop. No going out at all – understand?" she growled at them in a very loud, hard voice.

"We were going down to the bonfire to keep guard, just in case anyone tries to steal any of our wood," they all called back in unison.

"No!" Megan shouted at them again. "The bonfire is fine, you all stay here, and I will be back in 10, okay?"

"Okay," they all replied miserably and with that Megan ran out of the door with a shopping bag in one hand, and the note and the 10 shillings in the other.

Just as she got to the top of the slope which looked across to where the guard's hut was, a blue/green light was hanging in the air swirling around like a disco ball.

That's the portal, she thought. She ran down the steps straight to the phone box, picked up the little brown purse with the pennies in which she had placed in her bag (she seemed to automatically have it hidden on her all the time at the moment just in case) and shakily dialled.

"Hello," said the voice on the other end. It was of course Sally. "Megan what are you doing, did you get my note?"

"Yes of course I did. The portal, it's at the guard's hut," she said.

"It can't be we checked," replied a very flustered Sally.

"It is I am seeing it now."

"Oh, God!" said Sally. "Thank you, right leave it to us, do your shopping and get home as fast as you can, okay, darling?"

"Okay," she replied. She put the phone down, pressed button B, got another half penny out and ran down to the shops.

As soon as she approached the shops, she noticed Stuart's bike locked up outside the newsagents. It was about half past five now, and really dark.

What is his bike doing here? she wondered, as she ran into the grocer's store.

"Whoa, slow down," said Albert as she flew into the shop.

"Sorry," she replied. "Need Branston Pickle," she demanded, puffing as she spoke.

"Top shelf, middle row at the back," he said pointing.

"Great," she replied as she lifted the heavenly pot of pickle.

"One and six please," said Albert.

"One and six! It was a shilling 2 weeks ago," Megan retorted huffily.

"Price rises I'm afraid."

"Can I have a receipt please?"

"Yes of course," he said and gave her a slip from the till, and wrote on it Branston Pickle and signed it. He knew what her mother was like.

"Thank you, bye," said Megan.

"Bye," said Albert and started serving the next customer.

Then she ran next door to where Mr & Mrs Drew were just getting ready to close the shop.

"Just popped in to speak with Stuart, his bike's outside."

"Oh, love," said Mrs Drew, "Stuart's not here, he left ages ago with his wages and 2 bags of pick and mix, said he was going to meet his mates at the guard's hut. I am worried about that lad you know."

"Now, now," said Mr Drew, "the lad's all right, just not looking too good at the moment, not sleeping right he says."

"Oh well, I will see him at the bonfire tomorrow night and have a chat with him then, and see what's going on. Tell him I was asking about him when he comes in tomorrow morning will you please?" said Megan.

"Yes of course, love," said Mrs Drew.

"Thank you, goodnight," said a very worried Megan.

After running up to the off license and collecting a very large bottle of cream sherry, she made her way up the steps to the top of the slope and turned. The blue/green ball of swirling light was now tinged with red. She heard a growl.

"Time to go," she shouted out loud to herself, and ran up the road to the house.

Cold chicken, bubble and squeak, with Branston Pickle, and freshly baked soda bread, the 4 children ate with relish. Pudding was Ambrosia creamed rice.

"Sorry, kids no jam until the weekend, but I have put some ice cream in with it." It was devoured in minutes. "Everyone wash and get their PJs on; bed soon, so tidy up!" she called out to them all. Just as she was giving the orders the front door unexpectedly opened and in walked their mother and Megan went into panic mode. "Just washing-up and getting them ready for bed," she said to her mother with a really worried look on her face.

"Have they eaten?" her mother asked.

"Yes all done, just washing-up now."

"Uniforms?"

"Done," replied Megan.

"Okay, kids," Megan's mother roared, "everyone in the front room." They all ran straight into the front room and jumped on the sofa with worried anticipation. No one disregarded an order from their mother when she shouted like that. "The money." She looked at them with her glowing green eyes, took a breath and said, "The money, I have used it to book us a holiday next May, 2 weeks in a caravan in Weymouth." They were all in shock, and there was no reaction. "Well?" asked their mother.

"Hooray!" they all screamed with delight and ran towards her and without thinking, or normally thinking about it, hugged and kissed her to her sheer delight although she couldn't show it.

"Right, bed now," she shouted pointing to the stairs, which they all jumped up 2 at a time in sheer excitement. She grabbed Megan by the arm and asked, "Trouble?"

"Yes," she replied.

"I know."

"It's a portal, Mum."

"Are you absolutely sure?" she asked.

"Yes, saw it tonight on the way down to the shops."

"Do the witches know?" queried her mother.

"Yes," she replied, nearly dying with fright at the questions her mother was asking her.

"Bed," her mother said looking at her worried little face.

Megan obeyed, not wanting to get on the wrong side of her at the moment.

***

Earlier that evening, Mrs Green had rung Mr & Mrs Drew asking after Stuart and the possibility that he might still be there at the shop with them.

"Oh, love sorry! He collected his wages and usual pick 'n' mix for little Shelly, and said that he was meeting his chums over at the old guard's hut. Said he would be a little later than usual. I wouldn't worry, love," replied Mrs Drew. "He is the most reliable young man, he's probably just forgotten the time, I am sure he'll be home very soon now," she added.

"Thank you, Mrs Drew, I do hope so," replied a very worried Mrs Green, and with that put the telephone down. Fear and worry filled her head; this was just so out of character for Stuart. She knew her son really well, and had noticed he really had not been himself lately, blaming that bloody dog with the big yellow eyes, which of course, no one else could hear or see, for not sleeping. He always came straight home from the shop when he was working, with a bag of pick 'n' mix for his little sister Shelly, who was now sulking and making her life miserable, missing her treat of Monday night sweets.

Oh, God what is going on here? she quietly wondered. It was now 10 o'clock at night and he was never, ever this late, so she decided to telephone the police.

"Bristol Constabulary," was the reply from the other end of the line.

"It's Mrs Green here from Amberwell Walk, my Stuart hasn't come home this evening," she told him, tears creeping into her croaky voice.

"Right, ma'am," said the voice of PC Flower on the other end of the line, "try not to worry, but we really can't look for anyone unless they have been missing for 24 hours. How late is he?" he asked her gently.

"He is always home by 7pm every Monday night with his wages and sweets for his little sister Shelly," replied a now tearful Mrs Green, unable to hold back her building anxiety and emotion from this very calm policeman who was trying his best to assist her.

"I will make a note for the sergeant when he comes in, it'll be the morning now, and I will get him to ring you to see if Stuart has returned safely, but please try not to worry, we get calls like this all the time. I'm sure he will turn up."

"Thank you," she replied putting the phone down, but something inside was telling her he would not be coming home again, ever!

Chapter 16

Bonfire night

The next day seemed to drag for all of the children in school, because all they could think about was the festivities that would be taking place that night: the lighting of the bonfire, the fireworks and of course all the lovely food that would be on offer.

It wasn't just the children who were looking forward to it; everyone in the street was now getting very excited about bonfire night. This was a yearly get together for all the families in the neighbourhood, and this year it would be a really good one. The bonfire which already looked massive with lots of wood and furniture piled up high would become a beacon for the families who were working hard to make it the biggest and best bonfire around.

Megan's mother had taken the day off work to cook the huge amount of chilli con carne she would need to feed them all that night, along with making the chicken soup, cutting the onions ready for the hot dogs, and wrapping all the jacket potatoes in foil to be placed in the ashes of the cooking fire which she had already prepared. Megan had wanted to take the day off as well and help her mother, but her mother had insisted that school was more important, so with a heavy heart she made her way to school, thinking about the food for that evening.

School finished, and by the time Megan and her siblings had got home, everything was completed and ready to go. The air was electric and you could feel the anticipation and excitement all around. All that was left to do, was to get changed, cover the rabbit, and bring in the pets, and then transport all the food down to the cooking station that had been created during the day, about 100 yards to the left of the bonfire at the back of the allotments. The bonfire would get so hot it would have been unbearable to get any closer, so their cooking fire and food tables were positioned next to the drinks table, so it would be easy to serve the drinks and food without being burnt to cinders.

A large iron trivet was positioned above the specially prepared fire, and this fire would be used to re heat the jacket potatoes which Patsy had decided to cook during the day to make serving them easier, fry the sausages and onions, warm the massive cauldron of chilli, and keep the chicken soup warm as well. It was an old fashioned set up, and it reminded Megan of Ireland, because that's just how they cooked, and it brought lovely images and thoughts of the life she constantly missed. It worked brilliantly; her mother had part cooked the onions and sausages, and they would reheat and finish in a massive frying skillet perched on one side of the fire, leaving room for the cauldron of chilli, and the pot of chicken soup.

The plastic cutlery was wrapped in multi-coloured serviettes, the paper plates and bowls were stacked high and ready to use, and Branston Pickle, homemade coleslaw, a mixed garden salad, and grated cheddar cheese for the jackets and Daddies' red and brown sauces all adorned the groaning tables. The children all helped carry the food to the cooking station. People were already gathering, the hot punch was flowing, bellies were rumbling and the smells and aromas from the food teased the hungry revellers and the air was once again electric with excitement.

Megan's mother quickly cooked off some sausages and onions, and placed them in the soft finger rolls with sauce, and gave each of her children the first of the food, and told them to walk away so as not to attract any attention to the food, because she knew they would be really hungry, and at least she could get that into them until the rest of the food was ready.

Earlier that morning at about five o'clock, the phone rang unexpectedly in the newsagents shop.

"Hello, Mrs Green," said Mrs Drew the newsagent, "I take it Stuart didn't come home last night, his bike is still here, outside where he left it, I am so sorry. Have you contacted the police?" she asked.

"Yes, they can't start to investigate until 6 o'clock tonight, as that will be 24 hours since he was last seen," she replied.

"He could still turn up, love," Mrs Drew tried to assure her, feeling the other woman's utter distress and fear spilling out over the phone. "I'll ask everyone who comes into the shop today if they have seen him, and ask them all to keep an eye out for him, I'm sure he's not far away, and if we find out anything, anything at all, I will call you later."

"Goodbye and thank you," cried Mrs Green as she put the phone down.

"Dennis!" screamed Shirley Drew. "We have trouble. Poor little Stuart has gone missing and you will have to do the bloody paper round now!"

"Sodding hell!" he replied, walking into the back of the shop to where all the newly delivered papers were stacked and started to pack the green bags.

The bonfire was now well alight, but before lighting it, a thorough check for any wildlife that might have tried to make it their home was undertaken. Already some 50 – 60 friends and family had gathered around the burning beacon, lighting up the countryside, and throwing shadows around the bare trees and fields. It had to be one of the best for years, and large flames estimated to be 20 to 30 feet high danced out of the golden glowing pile, which spread a warming seductive smile on everyone's faces. The food was now flying out, the drinks table was already half empty, and everyone was totally engaged with the evening. Even neighbours who had not spoken for years became neighbours again, and the crowd slowly but surely became a family, as it did every year.

The fireworks were already started, giving spectacular shows of light and wonder. Big bangs filled the air and what seemed to everyone like a multi-coloured water ballet in the sky had everyone oohing, and ahing, and thoroughly entertained.

Two burly policemen pushed their way through the crowd with grim looks on their faces. Sergeant William Brown and PC Flower walked over to the food and drinks table, the crowd momentarily taking their eyes off the display to study the body language of the two policemen.

"Hot dog?" said Megan handing PC Flower a large soft bun, stuffed with a sausage and dripping in fried onions.

"Thank you," he said, taking the hot dog and stuffing it straight into his mouth, nearly choking on the oozing red sauce that trickled down the side of his lips.

"Nothing for me thank you, we are on police business," stated a huffy Sergeant Brown, whilst looking at PC Flower who was struggling to breathe with the hot dog stuffed in his mouth. Sergeant Brown raised his eyes to the heavens. "Oh forgive me, Lord for having such a prat as Edmund Flower as my sidekick," he muttered quietly to himself. "Stuart Green is missing," he announced.

"Oh, God," said Megan.

"Could you please ask everyone around if anyone has seen him? He was last seen leaving Mr & Mrs Drew's newsagents at around 5.30 yesterday evening. He said he was heading for the old guard's hut. I am sending my men around the estate now to check, but his mother is in bits, quite distraught, so if anyone knows anything or could give us some information, we would be very grateful," said the sergeant. He tipped his hat and turned to leave. "Edmund!" he screamed at the police officer who was now filling his face with half a baked potato smothered in chilli and topped with grated cheese.

"Coming, Sarge," he spluttered, chilli and cheese flying out of his mouth and spraying the sergeant with the remnants of his snack.

"Bloody buffoon," said the sergeant wiping his uniform with a handkerchief and walking to a police panda car which was parked at the top of the lane.

With nearly all the food eaten, the drinks table empty, and the fireworks nearly over, the bonfire burned brighter still, warming the air. The smell of sooty ashes filled the nostrils of everyone standing around admiring the handiwork of those involved. The last of the rockets were now due on. These were the biggest of all the fireworks and the families wanted to leave them to the last, as a special way of ending the night. It was always a race for the children to run around the fields and find the dead rockets the day after, and the one with the biggest rocket stick, was the winner. Consequently when these monsters of the night appeared, the children watched every movement of the lighters, so they could judge how the rockets were positioned, and which way they would fly.

The amazing rockets lit up the sky, and not only did they look beautiful, but their bangs and crashes could be heard miles away, that's how big they were. The ground shook under their feet, echoing the noise above, and it was totally exhilarating, just standing and watching the show of trails of fire in the sky. Sadly the last rocket faded into a memory, and everyone turned to say their goodbyes, and thanks for a wonderful evening, stuffed with food and satiated with drink and all very happy with the firework show. It was time to head for home, and for most of the children to go to bed.

Megan's brothers and sister had already gone back to the house, carrying the empty pots that would sit outside filled with soapy water, waiting to be washed the next day, a job Megan loved. It would be so easy; soaking them overnight would mean all the cruddy waste left over would dissolve and easily wash away. The paper plates, bowls and plastic cutlery were all collected and placed into black bags, and put into the embers of the bonfire to be incinerated in the scorching heat which made sure for all, that it was properly disposed of.

The sky suddenly went a funny colour, changing from a navy blue/black, studded with diamond sparkling stars, with wisps of smoky clouds floating around, to a murky purple/red, and Megan could hear a growl, a call, and it curdled her spine. She looked over to her mother who was dismantling the tables at the time, and who was now looking up to the top of the hill. Megan followed her gaze and nearly fainted on the spot. In the distance at the top of the hill was a massive pair of yellow eyes, big and brilliant almost like a pair of spotlights targeting them. A growl came again, louder this time, and angels appeared all around them like soldiers lining up for battle. Michael appeared in front of them both.

"Go now, quickly," he ordered Megan's mother, who was also sensing danger.

She grabbed Megan and throwing her over her shoulder, she started to run up the muddy lane which led to their road, and eventually their house. As she ran with her precious daughter slung over her shoulder, the sky lit up, and a massive thunderclap nearly deafened them. Heavy rain fell in shards, stinging them like little bullets. Another boom of thunder, and Megan then found herself at their front door, which was open, her brothers and sister screaming and crying with fright calling out to them as they arrived.

"What's going on?"

"Get in and close the door, I will be back later," their mother ordered fiercely, and ran down the street in the direction of the guard's hut.

They were all in bed and asleep when Megan's mother returned, suddenly waking Megan. She held her breath and listened. The growling outside had stopped, and the house was quiet. However, the minute her mother had locked the house and come upstairs to bed, the baby had started crying, and a minute later the noises on the stairs started again. Megan pulled the blankets over her head and tried to settle back down to sleep.

"Situation normal again," she said to herself as she drifted off.

Chapter 17

The day after

It was the day after Bonfire Night, and Stuart had not been seen for 2 days. The doctor was attending his mother and prescribing a sedative to help her sleep, but nothing really helped, and she just wanted her lovely brave boy back, her little man, her comfort and strength. He was gone, and she knew it, but 'why?' she kept questioning herself. Why him? He was such a good boy. Her tears fell like waterfalls.

"Let it all out," was all the doctor could say, feeling his own tears well up as he was comforting a very agitated and distraught mother. Why couldn't they find him? she kept asking, crying and talking at the same time, numb without answers. He knew this lady was hurting, really hurting, and he even worried at one point that her grief might drive her to try and hurt herself. She didn't see the hypodermic needle coming but she felt its effect within seconds.

The doctor knew Stuart as well, and thought he was a lovely lad, but death ran with life nearly every day for a doctor, something that touched them every morning they woke, and it seemed that this day would be no different.

Everyone was talking about their Bonfire Night, and how great it was at school the next day, but Megan was quiet, quiet in thought, praying, and asking questions in her mind, but sadly getting no answers.

"You look glum today," commented Mrs Evershott. "Did you have a lovely Bonfire Night?" she enquired. "I bet your food was good," she added, again trying to engage in conversation with a wide-eyed and teary looking Megan.

"Yes, but no," came the confusing response. "Yes the bonfire and the food were wonderful, and everyone said the food was lovely, there was absolutely nothing left, but one of our friends went missing 2 days ago and we are all worried," replied Megan.

"Oh, my dear, I'm so sorry to hear that. Are you good friends?"

"Yes," Megan replied. "I just can't stop thinking about his mum and his little sister Shelly who he loves so much. And his gran of course; she will be devastated."

"Well I am sure that the police are doing everything they can. Please try not to worry, and don't forget you have your cookery test next week. It's part of your CSE exam, so concentrate. Make sure your menu demonstrates skill. Making from scratch shows talent, and also an understanding of the chemistry involved in cooking. What are your thoughts?" she asked. "Oh and don't forget, you cannot spend more than £2 on your ingredients and the meal must be for 4 people," she explained.

Oh, God, where am I going to get £2 from? Megan wondered.

"Well?" asked a frustrated Mrs Evershott.

"Sorry," she quickly replied. *Bugger,* she thought, *think quick!*

"Well," said Megan grasping at straws, "I was thinking chicken liver pate (*Darren will help me out here,* she quietly thought) with red onion jam, homemade soda bread and homemade butter."

"Good, good, shows real skill. Next course?" asked Mrs Evershott again putting Megan under pressure.

"Well," she said aloud whilst thinking about the money side, "I could buy some lovely big chicken legs, take the bone out of the thigh, make a homemade stuffing, and stuff it, wrap it in smoked streaky bacon, roast it, and serve it with roasted whole carrots, cabbage, a leek and potato mash, and an orange and thyme gravy."

"Lovely!" shouted Mrs Evershott, "but I think hasselbacks would be better."

"Okay," replied Megan, "I will sort that out."

Once again the teacher pressed her. "What about pudding?"

"Well what about good old apple and raspberry crumble or bread and butter pudding, both served with homemade vanilla custard?" she replied.

"Got to be the bread and butter pudding," replied Mrs Evershott quickly, "never, ever tasted one as good as yours. Real custard though!"

"Yes real custard," Megan replied smiling at last.

"Good, that will take some beating," Mrs Evershott replied as she cleared away workbooks from her desk.

Megan was already working out in her head what she needed: the meat from the butcher, fresh veg from the allotment, fruits, ingredients for the bread, and the custard. She could hopefully use the frozen chicken livers in the freezer that her mother had acquired recently. She would also keep all the stale bread for the week. She was still adding it all up in her head.

"Could do it for about 10 shillings," she said to herself, frantically writing it all down, so she wouldn't forget. She would have to have a word with her mother, but 10 shillings was an awful lot of money to ask for, as that usually fed the family for 2 days.

As if we don't have enough to worry about already, she thought.

The police called on Mr & Mrs Drew that evening, and tried to piece together Stuart's last movements. They all sat in the shop with a cup of tea, waiting for the last of the paper boys and girls to return with their empty bags, so they could be refilled the next morning.

"I don't understand it at all," said a very tearful Mrs Drew. "He's worked for us since he was 7 years old. He has never let us down, always on time, the most reliable lad we have ever had, this is so out of character."

"When he left the shop that night what did he do?" asked Sergeant Brown.

"Well he came back, picked up his wages, took the two pick 'n' mix bags he always did on a Monday, it was his routine, one for him, one for his little sister Shelly, and asked if he could leave his bike outside, as he was meeting some chums up at the old guard's hut on the train line. We said okay and that was it, he left."

"Did he speak to anyone?" the policeman asked.

"Not that we saw," she replied. "He might have bumped into little Megan Murphy because she came looking for him a little while later. He's sweet on her," she snivelled back, whilst wiping the tears away. "Next thing I saw was him running across the road, over to the muddy path that leads up to the train line, and the old guard's hut."

"Did he go on his own, or did that bloody Murphy girl go with him?" he asked with a nasty grimace on his face, just as if he was thinking 'got you, you bloody Murphy witch'.

"No, he ran on his own, didn't he, Dennis?"

She looked over to Dennis who was quite concerned at the manner in which Sergeant Brown had just asked his wife that question. It was almost as if he had wanted her to say that Megan did go with him.

Bastard! he thought. "Yes, he ran across the road and over to the muddy path... on his own!" he replied sternly, making Sergeant Brown recoil, and look away almost embarrassed at Dennis' reaction to his question.

"Well thank you, you have both been a great help. I have already sent my men up to the guard's hut. Why the bloody hell South West Trains hasn't demolished the bloody thing I don't know. It's a bloody nuisance, and is just asking for all sorts of reprobates to hang out there and cause trouble. Anyway, they didn't find anything or anyone," he stated.

"Cattle have been dying though, Mr Pearce said this morning, and a horse was found dead in an adjoining field, both mauled to death," said Dennis.

"Really?" said the sergeant. "Nothing has been reported. Mr Pearce you say?" he asked.

"Yes," said Mrs Drew, "number 2 Watery Lane, the top estate, adjacent to the cul-de-sac overlooking the train line, and about 300 yards up from the guard's hut. He says funny things have been going on, and that it could even be witchcraft," she excitedly exclaimed.

"Thank you, Mrs Drew," a very frosty Sergeant Brown replied, "but I think that it is my job to ascertain what is going on. Our priority now is to find Stuart Green, and I ask you not to pass on gossip which is all it is at the moment, and completely unfounded. Good evening, folks."

"Good evening," said a very embarrassed and flushed Mrs Drew.

"We are off to speak with Mr Pearce now," said the sergeant and with that he got up and left with his sidekick, whistling as he walked to the panda car.

***

Megan had cooked the lamb stew the day before, as it always tasted better the next day. When she got home from school, she quickly changed and ran down to the kitchen to make the suet dumplings using self-raising flour, suet, salt and white pepper, chopped parsley, thyme, rosemary and sage from the garden, all mixed with a little warm water.

"Oh, an extra pinch of baking powder," she reminded herself out loud. "This will make you little beauties even fluffier." She took the lid off the large pot of stew slowly simmering on top of the stove, and rolled the mixture into little balls and gently placed them on top of the stew giving each one a bit of room to expand. "They will be about 30 minutes," she told herself.

"Yes, that's right," said the blue lady who suddenly appeared in the corner of the kitchen in her usual place.

"Hello, thank you for being here," said Megan smiling at her. The blue lady just smiled back. It never worried her seeing the blue lady appear, why should it, she had been a part of Megans life from the day she was born, and she always seemed to appear when she was cooking, just as if she was overseeing the whole thing, just to make sure it was always done properly, which of course it always was.

Megan then popped the soda bread mixture into the oven to cook, at the same time looking at the semolina which had already been in the oven for 10 minutes. She decided to give it a quick stir, and in theory, if she had got it all right, everything should be ready about the same time. The semolina would stand and cool, so it would be easier to eat, and she had already popped into the shops on the way home from school, and bought a jar of Hartley's strawberry jam, which had taken all the money she had left. She might have to borrow a couple of pennies from Sally's purse the next day, but the boys and her sister, always loved rice pudding or semolina with a dollop of jam, and when they were happy, her mother was happy. Well that was her little theory anyway!

Their mother arrived back from work, just as they were finishing their tea and Megan had already started the washing-up.

"Any news about Stuart?" her mother asked.

"No," Megan replied.

"Any bother today?"

"No," replied Megan concentrating on the washing-up in the sink.

"Makes a change," said Megan's mother speaking sparingly to her daughter as always.

"Mum," said Megan looking at her mother, "I have a cooking exam next week. I've already sorted out that I can use veg from the garden and the frozen chicken livers in the freezer. I'll also use all the stale bread from the week to make the bread and butter pudding. It's a £2 menu but I can do it for 10 shillings."

"Ten shillings!" her mother screamed back at her. "What do you think I am... a bloody bank?"

"Sorry, Mum, it's as cheap as I can work it out."

"Bed!" screamed her mother.

Megan gathered all the children, who were already washed and in their PJ's, and took them up to bed.

Chapter 18

The police come calling

The police were still doing their door to door enquiries. Stuart had still not materialised, and hope of finding him alive was fading. No children were allowed to play outside, and the roads of the estate were deserted. Even the local pub was quiet. It was as though a curse was hovering over them all.

The police knocked on their door just as they had finished their evening meal.

"Yes, Sergeant, how can I help you?" said Patsy Murphy, absolutely in no mood to speak to this evil man.

"I would like to speak to Megan if I may?" said the sergeant.

"Why?" Patsy's eyes glowed green and menacing. If there was to be any threat to her children, they had to get through her first, and it showed.

"Nothing to worry about, it's just that Mr & Mrs Drew said that Megan may have spoken to Stuart the night he went missing. May we come in?" he asked politely.

She opened the door wider. "Megan!" she screamed into the kitchen. Megan came running with a tea towel in her hand, wiping the suds off of a plate. "The sergeant wants to speak with you." Her eyes were glowing alarmingly and she was looking directly at Megan, as if warning her to be careful about what she said, which Megan acknowledged.

"Sergeant?" she politely replied.

"Mr & Mrs Drew have told me that you may have seen Stuart Green on the evening he went missing. Did you and if so what did you talk about?" he asked.

"I didn't see him," she replied. "I saw his bike and thought that he was still at the newsagents, but Mrs Drew told me that he had left some time earlier."

He again responded with his nasty look, his eyes boring deep into hers and his body language telling Megan that he really meant business. Megan's mother growled a low growl.

"Are you sure? Anything you can tell me may make a difference and help us find him." He spoke very sternly and came across quite hostile as he fingered his leather gloves and stared at the ceiling in apparent annoyance.

"I'm sure. I last saw Stuart on Friday evening. He said that he hadn't been sleeping very well."

"Did he say why?" he again pressed her.

"Yes," she replied.

"Well what the bloody hell did he say?" he again pressed, feeling exasperated, but not noticing that Megan's mother's neck had swelled, and her fangs were now almost visible. Her eyes were almost burning him, they glowed so hot green. "Well?" he again asked.

"He said there was a dog barking, and that he went to look for it to shoo it away, but never saw it."

"That's it?" he screamed at her.

"Yes," replied a now very shaky Megan, not worried about him, but terrified of what her mother would do to him if he continued speaking to her that way.

"But he must have said something else?" sputtered the sergeant, now losing the will to live. *What was it with this bloody Murphy family?* he was now inwardly screaming to himself, frustrated and irritated with the lack of information.

"That's enough!" cried Megan's mother, now almost bursting into her demon.

"Look sorry," replied Sergeant Brown, now realising that Patsy Murphy was standing taller than him. He suddenly felt very sick. "I really need to get to the bottom of this, it's as though he has disappeared into thin air. I just want closure for the family, especially his mother," he replied.

"He said that he was meeting his mates from the estate in the guard's hut, said they had been meeting there regularly every week," Megan said.

"Thank you, young lady, at last some information."

"Did he mention any particular friends?" the sergeant asked.

"No, he looked unwell," she commented.

"Unwell, how unwell?" he asked, curious.

"He said all he could eat for the last 2 weeks was sweets," she divulged, not looking at her mother, who knew exactly what she was saying.

Oh, God, drugs, bloody drugs, the sergeant suddenly thought, making him feel good that he was finally sorting it all out in his head. "It's all starting to make sense," he said wiping his brow, and winking at a clueless looking PC Flower. "Thank you." He turned to PC Flower, who now seemed to be in a world of his own. "Edmund," he bellowed.

PC Flower suddenly came alive, reddening from his neck upwards, and walking down the path towards the panda car with an enormous erection, and a smile on his face.

She's bloody done it again, the witch, God dam witch, bloody witch. "Station first," ordered the sergeant.

"Yes, Sarge," replied PC Flower, not looking at the sergeant, and struggling to get into the car without anyone noticing the bulge in the front of his trousers.

The Murphy children were all allowed an hour of television that night before bed. The local news came on and instantly a picture of Stuart Green appeared, with the police offering a reward of £50 for any information. No one said a word!

When she got up to her bedroom, there was a handwritten note on Megan's pillow. It was from Sally and it read:

Please ring when you can. I have a day off tomorrow. What about on your way to school? Be safe, love Sally, Elaine, and Claire.

Chapter 19

Father Quinn's visit

By the time that Friday came around there had still been no sign of Stuart. The whole community was stunned. Pictures of him and his family were in the local papers, and on the local news. Reporters from both, and even a national paper, were now trawling around, talking to local people, taking opinions and statements about the sight of the dying cows and horses that had been reported, and the missing dogs and cats. This was making everyone on the estate uneasy, especially Sergeant Brown.

On the way to school that day, Megan stopped at a phone box and got out her little brown purse.

"Hello," said the voice on the other end, "I knew it would be you. How is everything?" asked Sally.

"Well," replied Megan. "Still no Stuart, the angels are everywhere, and the police keep asking questions."

"What of you?" cried an agitated Sally.

"Apparently I was one of the last people known to have spoken to him, although Mr and Mrs Drew at the newsagents were the last people to actually speak to him."

"Oh dear!" said Sally. "That doesn't help. We can't see the portal, but you can. The 2 Archangels are coming to deal with it, but we need you to show us exactly where it is."

"Okay," replied Megan.

"By the way," Sally asked, "has your mother been going out a lot at night when there has been trouble in the air?"

"Why yes. How did you know?" Megan asked back, worried.

"We have seen her with the other one, you know, yours, trying to find the portal. It seems that for the moment at least, we are all trying to get this thing. Be safe, love, we all love you, keep in touch, bye!" and with that she put the phone down.

Oh goodness, Megan thought, *it will be a long day at school today*!

Friday was fish and chip night. It was always exciting going down for the fish and chips, because it always made Megan feel grown up in a funny kind of way. Tonight the fish and chips were as always covered in salt and pickled onion vinegar, and the children shared a bag of scrumps on the way home. Her mother had insisted that they all walk down together that night for safety. The community was still in shock over the disappearance of Stuart Green, and people were scared to be out alone at night, especially children.

Megan and her siblings ran as quickly as possible on the way home, trying not to spill the precious scrumps and it soon became a contest to see who could run the fastest and not spill any. Their mother was waiting for them when they arrived, with the table laid, bread and butter, and mushy peas already on the table, along with the obligatory red Daddies' sauce, and homemade tar tar sauce, which Megan adored. The children devoured the lot, while as usual, their mother ate in the kitchen, sat on her stool, with a cup of something.

Just as they were finishing and tidying away the plates, there was a knock at the door.

"Oh bloody hell, what now?" said their mother. She went to the door and opened it. "Father Quinn, what brings you here this evening?" she enquired of him.

"May I come in?" he asked. She opened the door wider and he stepped inside. "Oh the children are growing up fast. Hello, children," he said directly to them.

There was no response. Silence. No one liked Father Quinn. All he ever talked about in his sermons was the Devil, and Megan had seen him take both of her parents apart too many times when they were short of money and unable to pay their 10 shilling weekly contribution to the church. He would always turn up on a Monday night demanding it, taking the food out of their mouths, just to feed his wine habit. He was a nasty man and no man of God. Megan always considered him an evil beggar. He was the type of man who always had his ear to the ground, always asking for information from the neighbours, finding out nasty secrets about everyone in his parish. He probably found out from someone about the £50 reward money from the episode at the flat and was after some recompense for himself.

Megan remembered one night in particular, when he had made her mother and father open their pockets and mother's purse for the remainder of the money, and when they had proved they just could not pay, he left the house shouting out so loud that all and sundry could hear that they were a cursed family, and working with the Devil, and that God would punish them. What he had really been annoyed about was that he couldn't buy his usual 6 bottles of red wine, and a piece of topside for Sunday. Yes, he really was a very nasty man! Every time that she saw him, Megan had the very same feeling in her stomach. It was exactly the same feeling she had experienced with Harold Smith when she and Tinker were fostered by him and Sally, she always trusted that feeling, and unfortunately it proved right, and once again, it was back, just as big and just as strong, and she knew it meant trouble!

"Haven't had any contribution from you for some time now, Patsy, or seen anything of you at mass. Is everything all right?" he asked snidely.

"What do you mean?" she asked.

"Well there has been a lot of trouble around lately, with that young boy missing and animals dying. What do you know about it?" he questioned her.

"Nothing, why should I? I only know what the police are saying and what the papers, and news tells us," she replied.

"It's the Devil's work!" he screamed in her face, turning around and glowering at the children. He moved so close to them that they could smell the alcohol on his breath as he bellowed out loud and looked directly at them. They all recoiled from him except Megan. She could feel her hackles rising, and her throat thickening. "I don't suppose you have any money you would like to contribute to the church right now do you?" he asked, grimacing and licking his lips as he looked at the children with considerable interest. "I could say a prayer and absolve you all of your sin. Fifty pounds would be an admirable sum to contribute to your local parish priest and the church," he snidely spat at them.

"We have no spare money and are barely able to pay the rent, let alone feed ourselves. Tom is working away…" said Patsy.

He stopped her mid-sentence. "He is working then?" he shouted at her, and once again turned around to look at the children who were shuffling closer to their mother. "And earning money!"

"We haven't seen or heard from him for months. We don't even know where he is," said Patsy.

"Then how are you managing?" he screamed even louder, his eyes turning black, and rage building within him. "Are you being a little harlot, running around with other men for money? Is that how you are surviving in the eyes of the Lord?" he again shouted at her, eyes raging, and his lips parted and foaming in the corners. With his eyes fixed on the children, he suddenly grabbed their mother's arm, and again started screaming blasphemous things right up close.

Megan now exploded with rage. "You evil man!" she shouted at him. "Let go of my mum!" and then kicked him as hard as she could in the knee.

"Argh!" Father Quinn called out. "You little bitch! You're the Devil's spawn and I'll have you arrested for assault."

"And I will make a complaint to the police that you assaulted my mum, and that you are harassing her for money for your wine!" she screamed back.

He suddenly went very red. She was that close that she breathed in the vile stench of alcohol on his breath as he rubbed his knee.

That was some bloody kick, he thought. *I bet my kneecap is broken.* He cried out again rubbing his knee vigorously.

"Now get out, you evil priest, pretending to love and serve God and the church," Megan again cried back at him and pointing to the door.

"I will catch up with your father and make sure that he chastises you all," he bellowed back at them as he walked to the door.

"Out!" roared Megan again.

He turned and walked out of the door and down the path. "Bloody Devil family, repent, repent!" He was now shouting out as loud as he could for everyone in the road to hear. "I will go and see Sergeant Brown and get that bloody family evicted from that house and from my parish, and get someone else in who will pay their weekly dues, bloody cheeky brat. I'll phone the school and report her to the headmaster. Hic! Now where's the bloody car?" he said to himself as he wobbled down the road, hicc'ing as he went, totally full of the blessed red wine from his altar. "Sod it!" he said and went and knocked on the door of number 83.

A small, grey haired lady answered the door. "Oh, Father!" she said, very surprised to see him at this time of night.

"Mrs Bright, sorry to knock at this time of night, but I have been doing my daily visits and I have come over feeling very unwell. Could you possibly take me back to the church?" *I'll pick my car up tomorrow*, he thought.

"Oh dear, yes of course, Father, just wait a minute," she said as she went to fetch her keys.

Another sucker, he smiled to himself.

Megan's mother was incandescent with rage, and she slapped Megan hard across the face.

"Ow! What was that for?" she cried out.

Megan's brothers and sister cowered in the corner of the room, they knew better than to react or say anything when their mother was in a rage.

"Don't ever do that again," her mother screamed at her.

"Do what?" a bewildered and tearful Megan replied.

"Kick the bloody priest in the knee," her mother replied angrily.

"He deserved it," she cried back.

Her mother approached her ready to land another blow on the now sobbing girl. Megan suddenly felt her neck thicken, her hackles rise, and her fangs dropping. She was looking at her beautiful mother with glowing green eyes, gold wings and tail, and the three tell-tale golden bumps on the back of her neck. But her mother was also looking at her daughter, with her fangs protruding, glowing green eyes, little gold wings and gold tail, and the three little golden bumps on the back of her neck. Megan's brothers and sister had already run upstairs to their bedroom, fearing the worst, and closing their doors behind them. Patsy and Megan stood looking at each other seeing for the first time what had become of them both, their true selves, as they found themselves in a stand-off.

Just for one second, Megan stood looking at herself in a portal mirror. A massive electric shock went down her spine. Is this what she had to look forward to in the future? Is this what she would become? Just for that split second, an arrow of fear flew from her heart, straight towards her mother's, and a single tear, crept from the corner of her eye.

Never, ever in a million years will he ever get me, so that I am like her, she thought.

Patsy just stood there, reading her daughter's thoughts, and remembering the first time that her mother had seen her in full demon. Now the circle had turned in full, and here they were, mother and daughter, standing in front of one another, eyes glaring at one another, both quiet, and both very scared!

The very next morning, Father Quinn was sat in the council offices asking to see a manager. When the receptionist asked him what his enquiry was about, he replied that there was a family he wished to discuss who rented council property. The receptionist explained that it would not be possible to discuss the family's personal details or circumstances, as it would contravene the council's confidentiality towards its tenants. He replied that this family was causing trouble on the estate, and that they were part of his parish, and through gossips it had also come to his attention that they were in rent arrears.

In his opinion it would be better all-round if the family was evicted, and new residents brought in to raise the standard in the community instead of having all these troublemakers around.

What the bloody hell has this got to do with you, you nosey bastard? thought the receptionist as she was writing the slip.

"Sergeant Brown also agrees with me," he said.

"Well there is no manager available today, but your enquiry will be passed on. Would you like to sign here?" She pointed to a line on the form, on which she had made a little cross. "This will be passed on, so please make sure that your telephone number is correct, so the manager can call you, and we will be in touch. Anything else?" she asked smiling at him.

"No that's it thank you. But, someone will call me back?" he again asked intently, looking at her directly, and sneering a little.

"Of course, Father Quinn, but please realise that we are up to our eyeballs with work at the minute and it might take 2 – 3 days."

"That's fine," said a vindictive feeling Father Quinn. "I will look forward to it," he said smiling to himself inwardly. *Got you*, he thought as he walked away.

No you haven't, you nasty ass bastard, Elaine the receptionist replied inwardly as she heard his thoughts. *What is that evil bugger Father Quinn up to?* she wondered.

What was on her mind though were the Murphy family rent arrears which it seemed had once again been brought to her attention. The council had hundreds of tenants in arrears, some of whom would be evicted because they just couldn't pay, or did not try to pay or just couldn't care less, but the Murphy family had run into trouble when their father left. She was aware of the case, but had thought that it was all in hand, with the arrears being paid off on a regular weekly basis although she had noted some weeks that were missing, and lower payments that had been agreed, but all in all, the account was coming along nicely the arrears reducing, but not as quickly as they should, but still doing ok, so really there shouldn't have been a problem. The council never wanted to evict someone unless they absolutely had to.

She looked through the file, and realised that originally the debt was over £350, nearly a year's rent, but now it was down to around £200, which was still a fortune. Elaine had sat down with Patsy Murphy and planned a repayment scheme, which Elaine would keep an eye on, and in return for Patsy making weekly debt repayments, as well as the rent, she would keep the file away from the rent officer. He regularly asked to see the files of all the tenants with arrears, to see if any further action was needed. Patsy had kept her word and Elaine had kept hers, keeping the file quietly hidden away under the radar of the rent officer. Until now.

Elaine ripped up Father Quinn's complaint form and threw it in the bin when he walked out of sight. *I must ring Claire*, she quickly thought and did.

Chapter 20

Debt collector

Patsy had just finished the ironing for the day. All the children's school clothes were ready for the next school day and the bedding was crisp and folded perfectly, and just waiting to be put back up into the airing cupboard. The smell of the soda bread in the oven, and the succulent breast of lamb stew slowly blipping away on the top of the stove, which was waiting for the herby dumplings to be added later, filled the tiny kitchen. Woman's hour was on low, playing in the background as Patsy made her way through the remainder of her chores for that day, deciding that Megan could make the dumplings when she got home from school. She didn't know why, but hers always puffed up more, and they would fill the two hungry boys, who just seemed to be eating her out of house and home at the moment.

She sat on her stool in the kitchen, quietly fingering the large brown envelope that had arrived through the letter box that morning. The tell-tale sign that it was from the council housing department, was the stamp on the back of it. It was from the rent office in her area where she went to pay her weekly rent.

She could not understand why the council had suddenly started writing to her. No one in the rent office said a word as she passed over her weekly rent and the money towards the arrears in cash. She was up to date with all the payments, and hadn't missed one., well one or two when she was being pressured, but always tried to make it up later. Elaine, the housing officer, who she now knew was Claire Brannings' friend, had originally promised her that if she did not miss a payment and paid the amount due every single week, then no further action would be taken, and she and her little family would be left alone. She sat quietly questioning in her mind what exactly was going on in her life and why suddenly the council had started to get aggressive and threaten her. Most of all she wondered why all these bloody letters were arriving and making her once again feel agitated and very, very vulnerable.

108

She blamed that bloody bitch of a daughter of hers, Megan. Ever since she kicked that sodding priest in the knee, trouble had started coming to her door, and she was sure Father Quinn had something to do with it.

The hard knock on the front door suddenly brought her back to her senses.

Who could that be? I'm not expecting anyone today, she thought as she gingerly walked up towards the front door. Again, knock knock, came the sound from the door as it echoed around the small hallway, much louder and harder this time. Her demon let out a low threatening growl, which emanated from upstairs, and actually started to make the walls shake. Patsy tip- toed into the front living room and spied through the thick net curtains, trying not to move them, and give her presence away. She was almost holding her breath as she looked out at the tall man, who was dressed in a long grey gabardine raincoat, highly polished brown brogue shoes, crisp white shirt, dark blue tie, all topped off with a black felt trilby hat. He had a large wooden clipboard in his hands, a letter from the council in bright red writing clipped firmly to it. He seemed agitated and started looking around. Then he walked to the alleyway down the side of the house, but on seeing that the back gate was securely locked walked back to her front door, passing right in front of her as she watched him through the curtains. This time he knocked really hard and shouted out loud enough for everyone next door to hear, "Come on, Mrs Murphy, I need to talk to you about your rent arrears!"

Well, Patsy's hackles were instantly raised; how dare he shout her business out loud for everyone in the street to hear, especially that Mrs Nosey, Audrey Collings next door, who was probably already staring down out of her bedroom window, notebook in her hand, writing down all the juicy bits of conversation she could pass on to her friends in Kingswood?

She dropped her fangs, and let out a low, loud growl. The debt collector wasn't really sure what he was hearing, and again banged on the door and shouted through the letter box.

"Come on, I know you are in there, you silly woman!" he shouted even louder this time.

All of a sudden, a terrible pain ran through his head, and he instantly felt sick, and retched hard, bringing up his last cup of tea and digestive biscuits. He turned just in time and vomited it into a very large forsythia bush which nestled up against her front door but which actually belonged to Audrey Collings.

He fell to the ground, dizziness taking him off his feet. Again and again he retched. The contents of his stomach were now flowing out of his mouth, and all down his lovely smart gabardine raincoat, and all over his clipboard.

He was in total shock.

What just happened? he asked himself, as he crawled on his hands and knees down the garden path to the gate, finally getting to his feet once he was on the pavement outside. Feeling very foolish and very embarrassed, he ran to his car, which was parked just up the road, hoping that no one had witnessed that awful scene. After taking his raincoat off and putting it onto the back seat, he attempted to wipe himself clean with a hankie, whilst wondering what the bloody hell he had just been through. He quickly started his car, and drove home to have a bath as fast as possible, cursing Father Quinn for the little favour he had asked of him and making a promise that he would never, ever set foot in that particular house, or garden ever again.

Patsy stood and watched the whole event taking place, just outside her living room window. She now knew that someone was out to make trouble, and if he had come, then there would obviously be others coming to knock on her door. She would have to warn the children not to answer the door to anyone, absolutely anyone and as she was deciding this in her mind, her demon gave a loud, low growl. She instantly growled back, telling him to be quiet. She would handle this alone, and in her way, without any interference from anyone!

Chapter 21

Nigel Dickenson

Nigel Dickenson was Elaine's boss and he looked after the tenants for the local county council. He reviewed their rent, looked at tenants with rent arrears, set new rent rises, authorised repairs, alterations for the elderly and disabled, and yes on occasions, and only as a last resort, evicted tenants for non-payment of rent, noise, or damage to the council property. He was a powerful man, in a very powerful position, and he worried a lot of people. He was not one to be tangled with as Elaine had found out on a couple of occasions over the years they had worked together. However, they were a good team, and she always supported his decisions, but it constantly worried her that she never liked him. There was just something about him that didn't sit right. It was always his choice who was awarded the council property, and he would interview them like they were in trouble in a police station. When satisfied, he would award them the property, and it was Nigel that awarded the hard working Murphy family their property over 8 years ago.

"Good morning, I am Sergeant Brown, is Mr Dickenson available?" asked the robust man in police uniform with Brylcreemed short back and sides hair, and his police cap under his arm.

Elaine smiled and asked him to take a seat in her office, and left to go to Nigel's office, suddenly feeling very sick indeed, and she knew why. Trouble, that man was trouble, and it was headed towards Megan's family she could sense it.

Nasty vindictive bastard, she thought as she knocked on Nigel's office door.

She knocked twice and pushed open the door to see Nigel sat at his desk with a pile of files crammed full with what she thought could be photos, films on reels and loads of the new VHS videos that were now flooding the market,. Covering his desk, he jumped up, scattering the Videos all over the floor, quickly scraping everything together and piling it all into the massive cast iron

111

safe that sat behind his desk, cursing out loud at his own incompetence at allowing himself to be caught sorting his little side business out by his faithful and trusted secretary.

"Nigel, sorry if I made you jump, I did knock."

"Yes, yes," he replied looking very flustered, locking the huge safe with a loud clang and a large ornate key.

"Sergeant Brown is here and he wants to know could he have a quick word?"

Nigel's face contorted, displaying concern. "Oh, what, now?" he asked her.

"Yes, now," she replied. She suddenly saw something stir in her boss, a sudden nervousness. *What's he bloody hiding?* she wondered.

"Show him in," he ordered in an uncharacteristically meek manner.

Sergeant Brown walked behind Elaine as she showed him up to Nigel's office.

"Close the door," he shouted to her as she turned to leave the sergeant with him.

"Will do," she called as she closed it behind her. "Will bloody do," she said to herself standing quietly outside.

"I thought we agreed not to meet here?" said Nigel.

"Hello, Nigel good to see you again."

"Don't be bloody funny, William," replied Nigel in quite a nasty manner.

"I am here because we have trouble," said the policeman.

"What trouble?" asked Nigel now shaking visibly, and turning an ashen colour which matched the wallpaper in his office.

"The Murphy family, Bamfield Road."

"Oh yes, what about them?" Nigel asked.

"The young girl Megan, she's the one that was involved with our mate Harold's death. Then our other mate Robert Davies the ex-headmaster at the school, lost his job, and is on a suspended sentence. I couldn't get involved to help of course, as it might have uncovered us, but that's our little business 2 down, which equals £40 per month down in lost revenue," said the sergeant.

"What's that got to do with me, I just supply the contacts with their porn?" Nigel gingerly replied, looking directly at the now red necked sergeant.

"They have rent arrears I hear?" he questioned.

"How do you know that?" Nigel queried with quite an attitude.

"Because I'm a bloody police officer, you moron!" he now screamed back his voice getting louder. "I get to know everything. Nothing gets hidden from me. It's my job, and I am telling you that I want them out and get some new meat in. Father Quinn has just picked up a new paedo for us; he's getting them from the confessional. This is good business, Nigel, he absolves them from sin, and passes them on to us, and we supply the rest, but we can't afford to have anyone suspecting anything, or any troublemakers," he said pointing his finger hard into the desk.

"Okay, let's have a look," said Nigel. He opened his metal filing cabinet and pulled out a brown file. "Oh yes, husband working away, huge rent arrears, but being paid off weekly, and coming down very nicely. The mother's a real looker, if I remember rightly," he said not looking up at the sergeant.

"She's a bloody witch, that's what she is, and I want them out!" he screamed really loud at Nigel.

"Being a witch is no reason to evict this family, William, and anyway, are they a danger to us?" he asked.

"The young girl Megan knows too much, we want her out of the way."

"Okay, I will see what I can do, but I can't promise anything, leave it with me."

"I will be in touch," said Sergeant Brown as he walked across the office to the door. He turned around and looked at Nigel who still had his head in the file. "I expect to hear from you by the end of the week," and with that he left, walking down the corridor into Elaine's office. "Good day," he said to Elaine not even looking at her as he went out through the large double doors that led into the car park.

Evil piece of shit, she thought as she watched him leave.

Chapter 22

Rent arrears

Nigel Dickenson stood outside on the front garden path and knocked on the brightly painted yellow door.

"I'll get it," shouted Megan. She had just got home from school and was still in her school uniform when she opened the front door. "Hello," she said with a smile.

"Is your mother home?" the man asked.

"Who shall I say is calling?" Megan asked the smartly dressed man at the door.

"Mr Dickenson the rent officer," he replied.

Megan felt sick. *Oh, God*! she thought. "Just a moment please." She closed the front door and ran into the kitchen where her mother was busy preparing veg for that night's tea. "It's the rent officer; he wants to speak to you."

Her mother instantly reacted and her eyes glowed green. She quickly put down the veg and brushed past Megan to go to the front door, and opened it.

"Mr Dickenson, what do you want?" she asked him.

"Can I come in?" he politely asked. "We have a delicate situation," he added still stood at the front door.

"What situation?" Patsy asked.

"I would rather come in and discuss it if you don't mind?"

"I do mind," she replied. "What situation?" she again asked.

"Your rent arrears," he stuttered nervously, wiping his brow with a hankie from his pocket.

"They're being taken care of, and I am doing the very best I can, where possible paying them off every week as you have requested. You know my situation, I have 4 children here," she replied looking at this tall, thin, well-dressed man, with a very large briefcase in one of his hands and a large brown envelope in the other. Her eyes were now glowing a menacing green, as she sensed the fear emanating from him like body odour.

"Yes I know your situation and I am very sorry, but I have had a complaint from your parish priest that your children are running riot here in the community, with very unbecoming behaviour including taking furniture from old folks' houses and getting mixed up with bad council employees. We've also had other complaints from the neighbours about funny goings on here." He was now bright red and sweating profusely. He loosened his tie, and started to shake.

Just then Megan burst through to join her mother at the door. "It's not our fault that the council men stole all the money from the flat! We were only collecting furniture for the bonfire," she shouted at him.

Megan's mother grabbed her by the arm, and pushed her into the kitchen, and closed the door, giving her a nasty glare as she did, warning her to be quiet, which she duly obeyed.

"What has the parish priest got to do with my rent?" Patsy asked. "And what particular goings on are you referring to, may I ask?"

He was now soaking wet with sweat, and violently shaking, unable to look her in the eye as he spoke choosing instead to focus on the brightly polished red tiles on the hall floor.

"I haven't the time to banter with you, unless you can pay £200 in 2 weeks, you are all out, got it? I'm sorry, it's not my decision," and with that he pushed a letter of intended eviction into her hand. "Two weeks," he said as he turned and left, running to his car which was parked just 50 yards up the street. When he reached the car, he vomited his lunch all over the pavement. He felt absolutely disgusted with himself. *Bloody William Brown, he's always been a nasty bastard. I wish I'd never got involved with him. But if she does pay the £200 in time, there's no way I could evict her, no way at all, but oh, God, £200 is a fortune, she'll never be able to get that sort of money*, he thought as he started the car and drove away.

Megan's mother instantly pushed a ten shilling note into Megan's hand. "Sherry," she said looking at her.

Megan knew better than to say anything and made her way down to the off license, and when she returned, her brothers and sister were already sat at the table eating tea, whilst hers was warming in the oven. Her mother never spoke as Megan passed her the carrier bag and the change, and instead merely pointed to the oven. Then she unscrewed the bottle top, sat down and filled her cup, her eyes glazed.

Megan felt her pain, but said nothing, just taking her warmed tea from the oven: beef & kidney pie with a herb suet crust top with added cheddar, creamy potato and parsnip mash, cabbage and carrots, and gravy made from the stewed meat mixture. It was mouth-wateringly delicious as always, and her siblings were already mopping up the gravy with soda bread to grab the last remnants of taste, but Megan had suddenly lost her appetite.

Where are we going to get £200 from? she was thinking as she part finished her tea, leaving some meat and crust. "Chocolate mousse for dessert," she said to the chatty children now feeling very dispirited. It was quickly divided between 3 and gobbled up in flash. *Oh, God and angels please help us,* Megan thought and looking upwards.

Recently she had started to find her senses enhancing and she could now start to hear other people's thoughts and mind conversations. Her instincts were more reactive, quicker than ever, and once or twice, she even thought that she heard Sally calling to her.

I must phone her, she thought.

On the way to school the next morning, she stopped at the phone box and rang Sally.

"Hello?" replied Sally.

"Hello," replied Megan.

"Oh, my darling, how are you all?" Sally asked.

"We are being evicted because of rent arrears," Megan replied almost shamefully.

"Oh, God!" said Sally.

"The priest that had a go at Mum complained to the council. I think it was about collecting the furniture for the bonfire and all that trouble with the council men, and the neighbours have complained about funny goings on in the house. Oh, Sally, what do we do?" asked a very tearful Megan.

"Right don't panic, I'll have a word with Claire and Elaine about this. I have left a 10 shilling note under your pillow for your exam on Friday."

With all this going on Megan had completely forgotten about her exam.

"Thank you," she said still very teary.

"How's Mum?" asked Sally.

"Not good, quiet really quiet," replied Megan.

Not a good sign, Sally thought. "Right, young lady, you are not to worry yourself, the Lord and our angels work in mysterious ways. I know it's hard, but please concentrate as much as you can on school, and I will see you before your exam on Friday, okay?"

"Okay," replied Megan.

"Love you," Sally shouted out, and put the phone down.

Megan did something really naughty that day; she skipped her last lesson. It was art, and she always loved art, but she was worrying both about her mother and her cooking exam. She ran all the way home so she could go up to the butchers and the shopping centre to buy her ingredients, and get her bags ready for the exam day. It was her turn to cook tea, but by the time that she got back from the shops, she was exhausted, realising that she had not eaten lunch, so it was no wonder that she felt shaky and her legs wobbly.

It was cottage pie that night, with a cheesy leek mash topping, fresh veg, and of course, freshly baked soda bread. For pudding there was a lemon meringue pie with cream. She wanted everyone in bed, and everything cleaned and tidied by the time her mother came home from work. She mashed the potatoes with the onions and leeks that she had cooked all together, added butter, white pepper and salt, and a tad of cream, topping the mince mixture she had made at 6 o'clock that morning before she went to school. This gave her extra time to pop down the off license before her brothers and sister got home from school. She'd make the lemon meringue pie when she got back.

As soon as they had all finished tea, Megan rounded up her brothers and sister.

"Early to bed tonight," she commanded. "Mum's not too good, got a load on her mind."

"Oh!" they all responded.

"No buts, it's not her fault. Come on everyone." They all helped tidy and clean up, putting everything straight, just how their mother liked it. "Anyone fed Fudge today?" Megan asked. Silence. "Oh, God!" said Megan. Pulling carrots and lettuce out of the larder, she opened the back door and went into the garden, up a couple of steps, past the sheds, and through a small gate into the bottom garden. It was pitch black, and only the moonlight and the Winters' kitchen light next door, lit up the small and bulging vegetable plot in the back garden. Apart from that, it was complete darkness.

Fudge the rabbit had a cosy cage and run, just opposite the racing pigeons' loft, and Fudge was out in his run, looking for food.

"Fudge!" called Megan waving the juicy carrots and lettuce just in case he could see them. Fudge looked up happily, hopping straight over to her, with pricked ears, and making little squeaking sounds, which he usually did when he was excited. She opened the top to his house, and as soon as he was in, closed off the run, which also protected him from any foxes snooping around. She then dropped all the lovely juicy food in, which almost landed on top of him. "Sorry, boy, you must be hungry, I will make sure they don't forget to feed you in the morning," she said to him out loud while stooping to look around, and feeling very uneasy. There was absolutely no sound and no breeze, just a complete stillness. An eerie nothingness. The moon suddenly disappeared from the cobalt blue sky, a treacle like pressing darkness taking its place and starting to spread into everything it touched. She shuddered and a strong tingle went down her spine, a sure tell-tale sign of trouble, followed by a lurch in her stomach! *The lull before the storm*, she thought.

It must have been midnight, when Megan woke suddenly, hearing her mother working in the kitchen.

"What on earth is she doing?" she said to herself quietly, so as not to wake her sister who was sleeping soundly in the bed next to her. She could hear pots and pans clanking, and drawers being opened and shut. *She's cooking*, she thought.

Megan quietly got out of bed, popped a shawl around her shoulders and tip toed to the door. She opened it as quietly as possible, and with complete stealth tip toed to the top of the stairs. The kitchen door was open, and the aroma of cooking pies started to fill the bottom part of the house. She crept slowly down the stairs, avoiding the two creaky ones, and sat halfway down with a front row view of the kitchen, something she had done many times when her mother was cooking for a big event. Funnily enough, she knew that her mother knew she was there.

"Come down," Megan's mother ordered.

Megan did just that, and when she walked into the kitchen, the sight was amazing. In front of her were 6 massive pies, all freshly baked: 2 steak and kidney, 2 chicken and ham, and 2 ranch house pies, all steaming and bubbling and smelling fantastic. Megan nearly burst into tears with pride; her mother had been at work since 6 that morning, and she was still here cooking at nearly 1 in the morning.

"I have just done a deal with 2 local pubs. They are both starting to sell food lunchtimes and in the evening, and they have ordered my pies. What do you think?" she asked a very surprised Megan.

"Oh, Mum, you are amazing, I think they are fantastic," she replied with a large grin.

"Well I don't know how we are going to find that £200, but I'm not going

118

down without a fight. I've also written a letter to your father, but God only knows if he will get it."

"Don't worry, Mum, I know it will all be fine."

"Where did you get the money for your ingredients for your exam tomorrow, you didn't steal anything did you?" asked her mother.

"No!" Megan replied. "I borrowed it from Sally, and told her I would pay it back."

"Bloody witches," Megan's mother commented. "I wish they would bloody well keep their noses out, we don't do charity in this house," she growled at Megan, green eyes glowering.

"I can pay her back," replied Megan.

"Better be the last time," said a rattled mother, pointing to the stairs.

"Night," said Megan, and up she went to bed.

Chapter 23

Blodwyn's visit

There were very few times in the Murphy household when all was quiet, but when it did happen, everyone became happier, more relaxed and peaceful. It was at times like this that Megan and Trixie would be able to sleep deeply and restfully, without any babies crying, footsteps up and down the stairs and without their bedroom door handle rattling.

One particular week Megan got home from school and went into the house via the back door as normal. It was her turn to cook tea, and she had got up early that morning to make a start. As soon as she had heard her mother leave at 5am, she was up, washed, changed and downstairs, oven on, with soda bread made and cooking. It was Ranch house pie that night with a rich onion gravy, corned beef and onions with vegetables in a pastry case. She made the pastry and popped it into the fridge to rest, and quickly and expertly made the filling. She sweated a large onion in olive oil and a little butter, added chopped cooked potatoes, carrots and a drained tin of sweet garden peas. When all was nicely browned she added the chopped up tin of corned beef, 2 beef stock cubes, salt and pepper and half a cup of water until the mixture was thick and unctuous. Then she put it outside on top of the dog kennel, still in the pan with a clean tea towel over it while it cooled in the cold frosty morning air, which at that point, was much colder than the fridge itself.

When all was cooled, she made the pie. Two layers of short pastry, always half fat to flour were put on the top and bottom of the large deep plate, the edges were sealed with beaten egg, and the top was brushed and dusted with a little black pepper. It was then put into the fridge to cook when she got home later. The soda bread she had just made and was for breakfast to be eaten toasted with homemade bramble jelly.

I can make another tonight, she thought, boiling the kettle and stirring the porridge.

Everyone dressed and fed, they all left for school. Megan could actually relax a little that day, knowing her mother was working a double shift, so she would be home well after 10pm that night, which meant that Megan could spend a little longer with Mrs Evershott working on her menu for her cooking exam, which continued to worry her. At least Sally had lent her the 10 shillings she had needed for the ingredients, which saved her from having to ask her mother for such a large amount of money. It was hard enough for the family to live at the moment, especially now that her mother was doing everything to raise the £200 needed to stave off eviction.

Tinker, Trixie and Shamus were all home before her that day and dressed in their play clothes when she opened the kitchen door and walked in from the cold.

"What's for tea?" they all cried out at the same time.

"Ranch house pie. Now you lot go into the front room while I fix some tea and toast. Trix! Get the kettle on, love," she said walking through into the hall, and looking up the stairs, which momentarily made her tummy jolt like a little bolt of lightning, before eventually climbing them and going into her bedroom to change.

Downstairs she came, washed and changed and went straight into the kitchen, noticing the very eerie and unusual feel of the house for that time of day. The hairs on the back of her neck started to stand up, and she suddenly felt very cold. Looking around and feeling slightly wobbly, she could see nothing, but sensed something.

Have to be on my guard, she thought whilst at the same time asking her angels to be there for her.

The toast was smoking slightly under the grill, pushing an aroma of burning bread right through the house, making the children call out from the front room.

"When's the toast coming?"

"On its way," Megan called back, noticing even the blue lady was nowhere to be seen. Neither were the angels. *How odd*, she thought as she took the tray of toast and tea, along with Marmite and bramble jelly into the front room to satiate the hungry children until she could cook tea for them all later.

They piled into the tray of hot toast before she could even put the tray down.

"Hold on, you lot!" Megan cried out at them.

"Sorry! We are hungry," they all cried as she put the tray down with a thump, nearly spilling everything.

121

"You nearly made me spill that!" she commented very sharply, watching them greedily chomp on the hot buttered toast and sip their tea at the same time. "Tea will be at 7, if any of you are going out, back by 6.30," she commanded talking to them like a sergeant major.

"Only me out tonight," replied Shamus.

"Okay, love, please don't be late. Where are you going?" she asked making sure she knew where he would be.

"John Dyer's house."

"Okay, that's fine, but be back by 6.30 understand? If I have to come and find you there will be trouble!" she warned him with a very stern look, flashing her green eyes and making him wince.

He was back at 6.30, running through the door like a wild pony.

"Thank you, Shamus," she said smiling at him as he went through the kitchen on his way to the living room where Trixie and Tinker were watching the local news on the television. *Lovely boy*, she thought as he passed by. "Tell everyone tea will be at 7 please."

"Will do," he replied, not looking back.

Tea cooked and eaten, and the washing-up done, Megan got everyone washed and changed ready for bed. She pressed all the school uniforms for the next day, and cleaned and tidied the kitchen, so that when her mother got home from work everything would be ship-shape just as she expected it to be. As she was finishing in the kitchen, she suddenly and quietly started to hear whispers. She turned around expecting to see someone or something, but there was nothing there.

Strange, she thought, walking into the living room. "Bed everyone!"

"Oh!" they all cried out together.

"Come on, I am tired and Mum will be home soon, it's way after 9 now."

They begrudgingly made their way up the stairs whilst Megan tidied the front room, putting all the cushions in exactly the right place as usual. Again, she stopped. The hairs on the back of her neck were standing up, and a tingle was going up and down her spine. The whispers were back, and they seemed louder and nearer, but as she still couldn't see anything, she turned off the lights in the front room and walked quickly back into the kitchen.

That's odd, she thought. "Angels!" she called. Nothing, absolutely nothing. No one responded to her at all. "Oh, something just does not feel right tonight," she said to herself leaving a small light on in the kitchen for her mother for when she got home from work. She quickly checked the fridge, making sure there was a dinner put up for her, and then went upstairs to bed, checking on the boys before going into her bedroom.

"What's the matter, you are acting all funny?" asked Trixie.

"Don't know; the house is very quiet."

"Oh, God, not more trouble?" stated an anguished Trixie, starting to hide her head under the blankets.

"No I don't think so," Megan replied. "It's too quiet. Don't worry though, Mum will be home soon." She bent down and kissed her little sister, tucking her in lovingly. "Night, night," she said getting into her pyjamas, sliding under the bedclothes, and falling very quickly into a deep, deep sleep.

The whispers around her bed woke Megan suddenly. The room was really cold, and she could see her breath almost crystallising in front of her eyes, as she breathed in and out. A thin, grey, misty fog suddenly appeared next to her bed, before wafting its way all around the bedroom. The house was eerily silent, so too was outside. She shuddered, when suddenly right next to her bed where the fog was emanating from, a tiny speck of light appeared. At first it was a small fleck, but as Megan stared it began growing in size. Megan's eyes were wide with wonder and her spine tingled, but funnily enough she wasn't afraid. She didn't know why not, but she just sat looking directly at this growing cloud of golden light as it started to light up the room until it was so big, it touched the bedroom ceiling.

The room started to grow warmer, the light reflecting golden shadows which danced all around the room. Then it stopped. Out from the cloud walked a beautiful woman, about 5ft 4 inches tall and dressed smartly in a suit, with a collar and tie. Her hair was tied back into a bun at the nape of her neck, and dark red lipstick stood out on her beautiful face, highlighting her bright green glowing eyes. She wore a smile, bigger than herself, a smile above all smiles.

"Hello, Megan," she said looking directly at her.

Megan felt her eyes boring into her, but with a feeling of love, pure love. That was all Megan could feel. Love, not fear. Megan sat on her bed dumbstruck for a moment and then she noticed a large black mole on the woman's chin.

Where do I know you from? she silently wondered.

"I know you," the lady said still looking directly at Megan. "I passed when you were 9 months old. I saw you into this world, and you were taken to Ireland to live with your Granny Margaret. I have been watching you, and my Patsy too, but it's you I have come to see tonight, Megan."

"Oh my bloody God, Granny Blodwyn!" Megan called out, tears streaming down her face. "Oh, Gran I love you," were the only words she could utter at that very moment.

"I love you too, Megan," she replied now cuddling her to her bosom, and kissing her gently on the top of her head. "I've come to tell you that everything will turn out well for you in the future. I know it's hard now, and everything looks really bleak, but you are going to be fine, and please never stop loving your mother, she doesn't mean to be so cruel to you, it's that bloody demon in her you know?"

"I do," replied a smiling, nose running and crying Megan, cuddling the grandmother she had never got to know.

"We are all so proud of you, my darling, but I must make you promise me that you will not let your demon connect with your mind, however strong he calls you. Please promise me. It won't be easy, but you are strong, much more so than your mother."

"I promise," replied Megan, hugging her even harder. "But what about Mum?" she asked.

"Don't worry, me and Ma are watching over her, though we can't do a lot for her now, as she made her choice a long time ago, but we will be here to collect her when she passes. What we can do is make sure you stay safe and strong, Megan. You will be called to work."

"Work?" Megan asked, uneasily. "What do you mean?"

"Although you have the essence of the demon, my darling, you are a very special girl, a great psychic medium with wonderful gifts. You will be called to work spiritually when you are about 40. You will hear the bell and it will drive you crazy for a bit, but you do have free will. Your early life will not be easy, but you will survive and make it! My darling," she said looking directly into Megan's red puffy eyes, "why do you think you have so many angels around you protecting you? They are your friends. When you need them call, ask, always ask for help, if you don't ask you don't get! Remember that won't you?"

"I will, I will. What about Dad?" Megan asked fearfully.

"Well, he's the best thing that has ever happened to my girl, he's just struggling with himself at the moment. Never worry, he will never leave her, Patsy will make sure of that, but it's not your worry, concentrate on yourself and your life now, Megan. What will be will be. Can I give you a message to pass on to your mother?"

"How do I know she will believe it's come from you?" Megan asked tearfully, knowing that her beautiful grandmother was just about to leave her which gave her a little jolt in her tummy. She loved the sincere and warm love which emanated from this beautiful woman she had sadly never got to know.

"I will give you a special piece of information which you could not possibly know, and she will accept it. By the way, it's the anniversary of my birthday today," she chuckled, pulling Megan close to her and whispering in her ear. She then pulled away and said, "I must go now, promise me you will pass the message on, and keep strong you beautiful granddaughter of mine?"

"I will, Gran," she replied now totally overcome with emotion, and sobbing as her gran gradually disappeared with the golden cloud of light from which she had appeared.

The room returned to normal, and an angel instantly appeared in the corner of the room. Somewhere outside a dog howled in the distance, a baby started to cry, and footsteps could be heard pacing up and down the stairs. Then the handle of the bedroom door shook violently, making her jump.

"Oh God in heaven, back to bloody normal," smiled a now very contented Megan. Still fearful, she pulled the blankets over her head and settled down in bed, wondering for a moment if it had all been a dream. *God, wait until I tell Sally*, she thought, suddenly missing her cuddles. A couple of minutes later she fell into a deep and exhausted sleep.

Megan woke suddenly next morning, jumping out of bed in fright; she had overslept.

"Oh knickers!" she cried out loud, running to the bathroom to wash, before quickly dressing and running downstairs. She stopped suddenly in her tracks when she saw her mother who should have been at work, at the stove making breakfast.

"You're late!" she growled.

"Sorry, Mum," replied a cowering Megan.

"Soda bread!" Patsy growled again raising her voice menacingly.

"Yes," Megan replied quickly, throwing all the ingredients assembled on top of the worktop into the bowl, and producing a beautiful brown soft loaf ready for baking in minutes. She cut the top of the loaf in a crisscross with a sharp knife, and then quickly popped it into the oven.

"Mum!"

"What?" Patsy growled back to her looking up to where Megan stood at the sink washing the bread bowl, her eyes now glowing green with aggression.

"I had a visitor last night."

"Visitor, you silly girl, who would bloody well visit you?" she retorted looking back to the stove and the bubbling pot.

Megan gulped. "Granny Blodwyn."

Patsy froze and dropped the wooden spoon with which she had been stirring the hot porridge, spilling bits everywhere onto the floor.

"Don't lie, you little bitch," cried her mother clipping her around the ear as she replied.

"Ow, Mum don't," cried Megan. "She said you wouldn't believe me, so she told me to tell you that when you were a little girl you hid a dolly in a box under your bed. When you were paid £5 one night for a Ouija session with Ma Brunt, you hid the £5 under the bed in your dolly box!" Patsy dropped to the floor on her knees in the middle of the kitchen, tears howling from her. "Oh, Mum don't, please," said Megan. "It was the anniversary of her birthday yesterday," she said in a quivering, nervous, quiet voice, as Patsy sat sobbing in a heap on the floor, almost shaking with rage now.

"Why didn't she come and see me?" she screamed out loud, tears raining down and little puddles starting to form on the kitchen floor.

"She asked me to pass on a message."

"Tell me!" her mother screamed.

Half afraid, Megan walked towards her distraught mother, bent down and spoke the message quietly into her ear, just as Blodwyn had instructed her to do. All went quiet. Patsy got up, wiped the tears from her eyes, turned to Megan and said, "Tea, toast and porridge for breakfast, see to them for me, then get them off to school. I've decided to take a day off, so I'll do tea," and with that, she walked out into the hall, and up to her bedroom to reflect on her mother's message, which she now knew was from her.

The message was (be on your guard, Arthur is returning, me and Ma are always with you and you will pass on your 82nd birthday, free at last of the Demon, Thomas Jones will see to that)!

Chapter 24

The exam

Next morning Megan was up as soon as her mother left at 5am. She quickly got washed and dressed and was soon out in the garden, picking fresh herbs, parsley, thyme and sage, which she would wrap in wet newspaper and put into a plastic bag, which would keep them fresh until she needed them. She had taken the chicken livers out of the freezer the night before so they were already defrosted. She checked her list to make sure nothing had been missed or forgotten and gathered everything together, even remembering to let Fudge out, and give him fresh water and the remnants of the carrots and lettuce, which would see him through the day. Everything was ready by the time her siblings all came down for breakfast.

Everyone up, washed and fed, they all started to make their way to school as usual. Megan was now very nervous for some reason, but didn't really know why. She cooked all the time, but out of nerves she had checked and double checked everything that was in her bags before leaving for school. She headed straight for the Home Economics Department, where she would be able to put all her ingredients into the fridges that they provided until it was needed.

When she arrived at the cooking centre it was about 8.45am. The exam was due to start at one, so there would be no lunch for her today, as her last lesson of the morning did not finish until 12.30. She would need those 30 minutes to set up her kitchen and prepare. Her nerves were terrible and her stomach was lurching.

What on earth was it? she wondered. "Angels," she called, "help me."

All she heard back was, "Trust, all will be well."

Oh bloody hell, she thought, *another bloody riddle!*

"Hello, Megan," said a very excited Mrs Evershott. "All ready for a brilliant day?"

Mrs Evershott loved the exam days. Her students were the best around, and she always got very excited for them, pushing them to be the best they could be and more often than not, the highest marked students in the county, and today would be another good day! She knew it.

"Oh I don't know," replied a very sick feeling Megan. "I have a funny feeling about today."

"Rubbish! Stop worrying, you are the best cook in the whole school, a natural, and Mrs Brown who is examining today is lovely; she will love your food. She is a regular examiner and head of the local WI."

Oh, God I hope so, thought Megan nervously placing her food in her allocated fridge and kitchen for later. She then left to go to her first lesson without saying goodbye to Mrs Evershott, who was busy checking all the gas stoves that would be used in the exam, and setting up all the cooking stations, singing to herself as she arranged the chopping boards, knives and utensils that everyone would use. Every student's cooking station would have to be set up to an exact standard, and everyone the same. All students had to be given the same chance and opportunity, and she would make sure that they were. She was so proud of her pupils, she loved them all, and the marks they had achieved over the last 10 years always made her feel so proud and very much needed, and today would be no different. And of course Megan, her star student, would shine, and she, Mrs Evershott, chef, and home economist, BA, would take the accolade for it, which would get her even more noticed by Edward Scott, who she had a little crush on. He would surely pop by today and enquire how everything was going, and make her feel on top of the world as always.

Yes! Today was going to be a great day, she smiled to herself.

It was 1 o'clock, and all 12 students were stood, sweating at their allotted workstations, nervously looking at each other. They all stood behind their tables, with their brand new blue striped school pinnies on, recipes and timing sheets laid out on the stainless steel tables in front of them.

"Right, everyone, are we ready?" asked Mrs Evershott out loud, making sure everyone could hear her. "Let's cook!" she called out really excitedly, placing a large metal wind up clock on her desk for all to see. Once again Megan was almost rigid with nervousness, and couldn't move. She just stared at the table, groaning with ingredients, which were ready to be prepared and turned lovingly into something scrumptious.

Noticing something not quite right with Megan, Mrs Evershott walked down to her station. It was if Megan was frozen, frozen with fear.

"What on earth is the matter?" she asked.

Megan replied, "Don't know," unable to respond properly or even start to move.

"Right then, it's an attack of nerves. Start by looking at your timing sheet, and start with whatever needs chilling first," she said glaring at Megan and nodding at the same time to make sure she understood her little prompt. "Yes, coming, Geoffrey!" she called walking away towards a tall blond boy who was having trouble with his gas stove.

Megan suddenly reacted, her lovely blue lady appearing at her side.

"Hello, child, shall we start?"

"Yes," replied Megan still shaking, and holding the list.

The blue lady said, "Pate first." She was now pointing to the list, and it was as if a bolt of lightning had suddenly hit Megan as she came alive.

"Let's get going then," she said to herself.

Oh thank God! thought Mrs Evershott seeing Megan now actually moving and starting to cook.

Megan diced a medium onion, and a clove of garlic, and sweated it all down until the onion was clear and then put it to one side. She gently fried the chicken livers, but kept them still pink and a little bloody, then added them to the bowl of onions and garlic, seasoned well with salt and white pepper, and then added half a block of butter, fresh thyme and a splash of double cream, and mixed it all together in the bowl.

That smells wonderful, she thought.

Then she picked up a large sieve and with the help of a soup ladle, pressed it all through until a pink soup like consistency remained. She then popped it into ramekins, and covered it with foil, and put it into a water bath to cook in the oven for 25 minutes on a high setting. When it cooled it would be popped into the fridge to set. She would then put clarified butter on along with a little sprig of fresh thyme about 20 mins before the end of the exam.

Bread and butter pudding was next. She buttered the oval Pyrex dish, and dusted it with sugar, then layered slices of bread that had been buttered on both sides, sprinkling that with tea soaked sultanas and raisins, sugar nutmeg and grated orange rind and layered it until the dish was full. Four large eggs were then beaten and mixed with one pint of double cream, and topped with a little milk, which was then added, and squashed down so the bread absorbed all the liquid. She would cook the pudding later. She now had time to prepare the hasselback potatoes and fresh veg, then the gravy.

Great, she thought, *I am now back on track.*

Louise Brown was a lady of very high standing in the community. She was married to Sergeant William Brown, who was at this moment in time, vigorously stamping his authority on his new patch, and very proud of him she was too! She was the head of the local Women's Institute, and had become a cookery examiner for the local schools 3 years ago, at the request of the W.I. It was all voluntary of course, but she could claim her travelling expenses and overnight stay, if she had to stay locally. Now Louise always produced an invoice for the school when she was examining, and claimed mileage and a night's stay at a local hotel. This was strange as she only lived 5 miles away from the school, but no one ever questioned her honesty as she was married to the local police sergeant.

Louise ran her branch of the local W.I. with a rod of steel. Jams, chutneys and sponges were her forte. She had won more rosettes and awards for her locally produced fayre than any of the other members in the branch, and as she was brought up on a farm, she had learned to cook at an early age, because just like Megan, she had to. On the farm you worked like a team, and she of course was the leader.

She arrived exactly one hour before the end of the exam. This was quite usual. She would then sit with Mrs Evershott and over a cup of tea, go through each student's menu, then proceed to walk around and watch them at work, stopping sometimes to chat and ask questions. Jean and Louise sat sipping tea, chatting and catching up, but also checking each menu, smiling to each other as they sat in the two soft chairs at the end of the classroom.

"Well this all sounds and looks wonderful today," said Louise. "Two especially stand out to me. Timothy Taylor's hand breaded lemon sole goujon starter, braised guinea fowl and chocolate Crème Brulee topped with gold leaf, sounds wonderful and if he pulls that off, that could be fab," she excitedly commented to Jean. "But this one I particularly like," she said handing Megan's menu over.

"Yes, we all love this young girl; she will go far hopefully, if I can persuade her to become a chef. She's got the makings of a brilliant one. Shame she's got it so hard at home though. Her mother is a bully and a nightmare. Talk about turning a pig's ear into a silk purse. She works miracles with all the cheap cuts of meat you know, uses stuff I would never think of," replied the very proud teacher.

God! Louise suddenly thought. *This is the bloody girl William has been creating about, and making my life very miserable over. This is the girl who is threatening his outside business. I'll bloody well fix her.* A nasty grimace suddenly appeared on her face. "Right then, Jean, let's go walkabout and start looking at our students' cooking." She smiled broadly, as she walked down the classroom towards them all.

With the pate finished and nicely topped with clarified butter and a twig of fresh thyme, stuffing the prepared chicken legs was quick and easy, as Darren the butcher had taken the thigh bone out for her already. She gently bashed the thigh meat which was still attached to the drum end of the leg, spread it open, filled it with her usual stuffing, which she had already made, and wrapped the bashed meat around it, and wrapped the whole thing in smoked streaky bacon, which she thinned by gently running a palette knife along the rasher, making it more economical. The hasselback potatoes were already prepared, and brushed with a mixture of melted butter and olive oil, salt and freshly milled black pepper, and a sprinkling of chopped fresh rosemary. The carrots she decided not to roast but to steam with the cabbage, giving a fresher flavour and the orange and thyme gravy was already bubbling nicely.

Louise left Megan until the last. "Plate up now, everyone, 5 minutes left," shouted Mrs Evershott. Louise walked up to Megan's station, just as she was starting to plate everything up. Megan instantly shook, a bolt of tingle flying up her spine and an unpleasant feeling in her gut.

"Think you can cook do you?" Louise scowled at Megan looking at her with a nasty satisfied expression on her face which suggested a deep maliciousness. Then looking down at the plated food she thought, *Oh, God, that's bloody amazing.* Then she turned around and walked away leaving Megan still shaking, and her tummy telling her something was off.

All the students were now asked to leave the classroom so that Mrs Evershott and Louise Brown could judge and taste, and then mark their efforts for the finished results. Instantly Jean Evershott felt that Louise was different today, making spurious remarks about every student's dish that they tasted.

Not like her, thought Jean.

"Yes, lovely, lovely," said Louise about an apple pie that was totally undercooked, its pastry raw and soggy on the bottom. She then awarded the student a B, which really should have been a D-.

What's she up to? Jean thought feeling her hackles rise. *She's totally randomly marking students, this isn't Louise.* "Louise," said Jean, "are you okay?"

"Yes, why?" she replied.

"I don't actually agree with the last set of marks you have just awarded," but just as she was about to get nitty gritty with her, the door to the cooking department opened and in walked the headmaster, Mr Scott.

"Don't mind me, ladies," he said, "I always love to come and see how the students have done. My wife's a bit of a cook you know. Carry on!" he said walking round and tasting and inspecting the food.

The students had worked very hard today, he had decided, but two stood out as the best of the day. Timothy Taylor's and Megan's food was absolutely exquisite, both AA standard. He really could not choose between them, the only difference was that Tim Taylor was 15, and Megan was 10 and a half. Mind you, in all the restaurants he had ever been to, no one had ever given him toasted soda bread with pate, and bread and butter pudding that tasted that good, it was sublime. He smiled to himself as he left the classroom, and popped next door into the art room.

Jean was quite fraught and angry by the time she and Louise got to Megan's station. Everything was quite beautifully presented and although you could see that the headmaster had nibbled the food, it still looked amazing.

"Oh no," stated Louise Brown, "what sort of presentation is this? How very disappointing."

"Modern and innovative," replied Jean. "This is wonderful work."

"No, no," stated Louise as she tasted the pate. "No brandy in the pate."

"I don't think you need it," replied Jean, "it's quite delicious and anyway this young girl only had 10 shillings to cook the whole meal with, and she's cooked all this with practically nothing. All the other students had £2."

"I am quite aware of the content and requirements of the exam paper, Jean, but quite honestly if you can't afford proper food, don't do the exam," stated Louise.

"What!" screamed a very revved up and by now exasperated Jean Evershott. "Are you saying that people from poor families can't take exams?"

"No of course not," replied a very reddening Louise, "but honestly, stuffed chicken leg, I ask you, who eats chicken leg today?"

"I bloody do," screamed Jean. "And this is fantastic; you wouldn't know it was a stuffed chicken leg if you hadn't read the bloody menu."

"The custard is far too thin as well," Louise retorted nastily, looking the other way.

"Louise! It's Crème Anglaise, it's meant to be thinner."

"C –,"said Louise as she signed off the form and gave a copy to Jean, "and she had better think herself lucky at that," she added, glaring into Jean's reddened mad eyes.

Louise Brown stomped out of the classroom with the sealed brown envelope under her arm, as she headed for the school office with her invoice for her expenses, which if she asked nicely, they would pay today.

"Gotcha," she said to herself smugly as she walked down the corridor.

The phone in the cooking department rang, as Jean was standing there almost in tears, asking herself what had just happened.

"What?" she screamed down the phone in anger.

"Jean, it's Sally."

"Oh, Sally, hello. Sorry, we have just had the most terrible exam."

"Oh goodness, that's why I was ringing. How did Megan get on?" she asked worriedly.

"Disastrously," replied Jean. "C-, the examiner hated her food. She said if you could not afford to buy proper food, don't take the exam." Jean was now crying softly, totally embarrassed and feeling very hurt with the day's events.

"Fucking bitch!" screamed Sally.

"Yes," said Jean, "she has been examining here with me for the last 3 years, a lovely woman, Louise Brown. She's married to the sergeant who is now in charge of the whole local constabulary. I am so upset, Sally. Megan was so nervous, she froze, but went on to cook the best I've ever had the privilege to see, and the food was truly wonderful."

"What's the bitch's name again?" screamed Sally down the phone.

"Louise, Louise Brown."

"Oh, God, it all makes sense, he's the nasty bastard that has got it in for Megan's family. He's trying, along with the parish priest, to get them evicted next week. There's more to it. Please, Jean, tell the headmaster," and then she proceeded to fill her in with the situation that was unfolding.

The conversation finished.

"Oh goodness, I must find Mr Scott," she said out loud to herself, and just out of the corner of her eye, saw him leaving the art class next door. "Mr Scott, do you have a moment, I have a very urgent situation you need to know about?"

When they had finished their conversation a short while later, Mr Scott said, "Okay, let's deal with this lady." He picked up the telephone and dialled the office. "Hello, Judith it's Ed here, is Louise Brown in the office?" he asked.

"Yes, Ed," she replied, "just waiting for her cheque."

"Oh lovely," replied the headmaster. "Do me a favour, slow everything down will you? Give her a cup of tea or something; I want a word with her. Don't give her the cheque until I get to the office, okay?"

"Yes fine, Ed, no worries." *Oh, what's all that about*? she wondered as she got up from her desk and walked into the finance office. "Gill, is Louise's cheque ready?" she asked.

"Just coming," replied Gill the school cashier and treasurer.

"Well don't give it to her yet, Ed wants us to delay her. He wants a word with her, okay?"

"Okay," replied Gill. "Get her a cup of tea would you please, Josie?" Gill called out to a young girl sat in the office on the computer.

"Okay," Josie called out as she put the kettle on, and got a cup and saucer ready.

Gill raised her eyes at Judith. "Wonder what that's all about then," she remarked.

Louise found a comfy chair in the office, a cup of hot steaming tea and two digestive biscuits later, she was feeling a little better, *"no need for a snack when I get home"* she thought to herself as she gazed quietly around the plain white walls of the office waiting room, they were adorned with plaques and award certificates from various sports, such as athletics and football and of course displayed with pride. She noticed a large vase of flowers starting to wilt on the large bright windowsill opposite, "they won't last long" she thought to herself, noticing the large thick python like radiator pumping out heat below, they didn't stand a chance being hit with heat from below and the bright sunshine from above, making the room seem clammy and dry.

"Oh come on," she again spat the words out quietly as she sat now starting to feel quite uneasy, "why are they making me wait? I never wait" she told herself, a little panic now starting to creep in. Thinking back to the time when William was appointed Sargent, and she was invited to be the regular judge for the cooking exams over 3 years ago, her own W. I. group were overwhelmed with pride that she had got the job.

It was over 3 years ago that Louise and William stayed in a lovely little hotel just on the outskirts of Bristol, not far from Henlade School, just some 3 miles away, when he was called for his interview for the position of Sargent, which of course later, he was offered, appointed not long after. After a lovely nights stay, she settled the bill at the reception desk in cash and asked for a card. The food was good, rooms lovely and comfortable, and the ambiance of the place very relaxed; she was actually thinking that this would be a nice place to meet up with her lady friends who liked to lunch once every month "umm yes, I think we could meet up here" she told herself looking around the opulent and inviting surroundings.

Alas, the hotel had actually run out of business cards, but the quick thinking and very professional receptionist who did not want the hotel to miss out on another possible regular guest gave Louise a blank invoice sheet, which had the name and address of the hotel, the phone and fax number as well, just in case she needed to call to book a room or reserve a table, in fact it was the very same invoice sheet the receptionist had just hand written and signed in receipt for their nights stay; and not really thinking anything anymore of it at that moment, she folded the plain invoice sheet, and carefully popped it into her W. I. briefcase which she carried with her everywhere, and returned home happy with William that very day.

The kindly and very handsome Edd Scott who had interviewed Louise for the position of Examiner, had told her that although there would be no payment for the actual work of judging the examination, the school would be very pleased to pay for any expenses she incurred judging for the school, they felt it only right, including an overnight stay if she had to, as long as an invoice was produced to the office staff. Well you can imagine what thoughts were running riot through Louise's head; at that particular time, William was keeping her very short of money to spend, his little sidelines were slow, and business poor, and he was always so aggressive and nasty when she asked him for a little top up in her bank account; "I'll show you that I can earn money myself you nasty swine" she thought; she still had Williams original bill in her briefcase, and the signature of Jenny Jones, was really easy to copy; also being very careful to phone the hotel every now and again just to make sure Jenny Jones still worked there, and what the nightly rates were. After attending a W.I. meeting in Dorchester one day, she popped into their office and asked very nicely if she could use the photocopy machine, and stood there quietly photocopying 20 copies of the plain invoice, and that was it! Every exam day like today, when she had finished marking and judging an exam, she would hand over her expense sheet, with a like for like copy every time of the Manor Hotels bill, attached, "easy" she always thought; no one had ever questioned or queried her bill, always thanking her for her professionalism in her judging and her paperwork, making the office staff lives much easier her cheque was always paid that same day, yes it all always went so smoothly, and Louise's bank account swelled nicely; She didn't have to ask William for any extra money now, she dined out with the best male escorts that money could buy for sex and company, William didn't mind, why should he, his sexual preferences were elsewhere, she could now afford it, and quite frankly it kept her sane, yes life at this moment in time was very very good, she had everything in life she wanted (well almost everything!) and she had a nice steady regular income, well that was until today! Something she felt wasn't quite sitting right, she could feel it, but she had got that nasty little brat that was making Williams life unbearable good and proper, a sly smile passed across her face at the thought of what she had just done, "perhaps his little businesses would now take a turn for the better, now that she was out of the way" she told herself, now thinking of the next holiday abroad, and her new car that was due soon, "yes Barbados, Barbados" it would be this time she smiled to herself as she still sat and waited for her cheque.

Meanwhile Judith just shrugged her shoulders and walked out of Edds and back to her office, to go and tell Louise another cup of tea would be coming while she was waiting for her cheque.

Louise Brown was still sat in a soft, comfy chair in the office sipping her fresh tea, while leafing through a magazine that was placed on the coffee table in the middle of the room, she was feeling really nervy and irked that she had been left waiting around for so long, she might just make it in time to the bank if they paid her now she was thinking to herself.

"Ah, Louise," said Ed Scott as he walked up into the office. "Good day in the kitchen?" he asked.

"Yes thanks," she replied smiling.

"Do you have the exam board envelope?" he asked her.

"Why yes of course. I will take it straight to the post office when I leave here and make sure it goes 1st class."

"Oh that won't have to happen, I have the GPO picking up the other exam results today, it's a special pick up that the school has paid for, they can all go together, and that will save you some postage," he said smiling at her, as he held his hand out to receive the envelope.

"If you are sure, Headmaster. I always take it myself," she replied and begrudgingly handed it over.

"Thank you," he said, taking the brown envelope into the office and closing the door behind him.

He picked up the phone and dialled.

"Yes, Ed?" said Judith.

"Send her cheque in the post, and get rid of her now."

"What about the exam list for her next assessment, she's due to judge 7 more exams in the coming months?"

"Tell her we'll let her know as all the information hasn't been collated yet," said the headmaster.

"Will do," she replied and proceeded to deal with Louise Brown. *What have you done to upset Ed?* she wondered just before she gave Louise the bad news that the cheque, along with the dates she had asked for would arrive in the post. A disgruntled Louise finished her tea, and stomped out of the office down to the car park where the bright red Mercedes Benz waited for her.

Megan and her fellow students were now allowed back into the kitchen to collect their cooked food and clean their cooking stations down. She had brought 3 large Tupperware containers to take her food home in, and packed and cleaned in silence. In fact no-one spoke. Every one of the students had been so nervous, their nerves were frazzled and they were all mentally exhausted.

As soon as she reached the school gates on the way home, Megan heard a "Yoo Hoo." It was Sally. "Come on, m'girl, I will give you a lift home."

"Oh thank you," Megan replied getting into the car.

"I was just passing, how did today go?" she asked.

"Okay I think."

"Well I am sure that you did brilliantly, it all smells wonderful, and is making my mouth water," Sally said smiling before pulling away and heading for Megan's house. "Any more news from the council?"

"Nothing," replied Megan.

"Well now, don't worry; it'll be fine I know it."

"I hope so," said Megan, "Mum's really worried."

Sally drove on. "You know, Megan, I just know, I don't know how, but I know it will all be okay," Sally said assuredly, this time looking at Megan while they were stopped at traffic lights. "Trust."

"I will," she replied.

They drove on in silence.

Headmaster Ed Scott sat at his desk and opened the brown envelope which was addressed to the South of England Examination Board in Exeter. He pulled out the results sheets and checked through the examination grades.

"Let's see what you have been up to," he said to himself out loud. Mr Scott had looked at and tasted every student's finished dishes. For him it was one of the perks of the job, and being that he considered himself a bit of a cook, had himself judged the cooking exams until Louise Brown had come along, very highly recommended from the W.I., which then in turn gave him more time for his headmaster duties. But today had been a very good exam, with only 2 students failing to finish on time, and another 2 whose dishes were not quite cooked enough, but what he was reading didn't make sense. The two who did not finish in time were given B's, instead of what probably should have been D's, and the two with the uncooked dishes had been given B+, when it should have been C-. It should also have been the older boy Timothy Taylor, whose food was on par with Megan's, but he had a B-. "I think I had better re-score these," he said to himself out loud, and then he noticed that there was actually no score at all for Megan. An original C- had been rubbed out and an F for fail was now in the box. "Last time you work for us," he murmured changing Timmy Taylor's mark to an A. "And you young lady, will also get an A," he said once again speaking to himself out loud. He checked through all the other paperwork, amending as required, then put the forms back into the envelope, sealed it and walked into the office. "First class please, Judith."

"Righto," she replied.

"Could I also have Louise's invoices please?"

"Yes of course," Judith replied handing him a typed paid invoice with a cheque stapled to it.

"Send the cheque 2nd class, I'll keep the invoice," he said taking the cheque off and passing it back. He turned around and walked back into his office.

God, what is going on, he's acting weird today? Judith again thought, as she placed the cheque into an addressed envelope.

Mr Scott sat at his desk and pulled out a file on Louise Brown. It held all the invoices that the school had paid her over the last 3 years. Thirty-six exams she had judged, each time producing an invoice for services rendered. Her hotel bill, evening meal and mileage expenses were always about the same, coming to around £120 per exam. Multiplied by 36 it amounted to £4,320, a small fortune, and all paid by the school out of the school fund. It was never questioned, but Ed was very upset with today's skulduggery, and for the first time, wanted to question her invoice.

He picked up the telephone and dialled the number.

"Manor Hotel," a very posh female voice replied from the other end.

"Oh hello, I wonder if you can help me, we had one of our examiners stay with you last night, and she's left her handbag, and I was just wondering whether she had checked out yet, as I would like to get it to her."

"Who's calling please?" the very posh voice enquired.

"Ed Scott, headmaster of Henlade School."

"What's the person's name?" she asked.

"Louise Brown."

"No guest registered in that name stayed here yesterday evening," the receptionist replied.

"Are you sure?" he asked. "She's been staying with you on a regular basis over the last 3 years," he exclaimed.

"I can assure you, Headmaster, I have worked here for the past 10 years, and I would have remembered a regular. We have many, and I know them all, and a Louise Brown has never to my knowledge stayed here."

"Could you check the 20th of October for me as well?" he again asked, as this was the last invoice they had paid.

"No Louise Brown stayed with us on that date," she again replied.

"You know I might well be ringing the wrong hotel, I am so sorry to have bothered you, silly me, thank you so much for your help," he said and put down the receiver. This was the last time Louise Brown would ever set foot in his school again, he decided there and then.

He had Judith his secretary write a letter, that would now accompany the cheque thanking Louise for all of her hard work over the years, but advising her that her services were no longer required due to reduced school funding. He also had Judith add a very important item to the agenda of the next school AGM, which was being held the following Monday evening. Item 12 would discuss ways to raise money for a special fund specifically to be used to help poorer students with exam expenses.

Chapter 25

Confronting your demons

It was 2am the next morning, and it had been an unusually quiet night so far, with no crying baby, or footsteps up and down the stairs, or any angels around. Megan was in a light sleep when her mother woke her, shaking her gently.

"We need you with us tonight; we're going to the portal. Dress warm, it's cold outside. The angels are coming to babysit your brothers and sister, so don't worry. Quickly now," and with that she left her to go downstairs to wait.

Megan dressed quietly and quickly saying a prayer to ask for protection for whatever was going to happen that night, and then joined her mother downstairs. They left quietly out of the back door, putting the large backdoor key inside the dog kennel for when they returned.

Her mother never spoke a word to her and instead just started running down the road. Megan followed after her, and was amazed that she could actually keep up. Down the slope they went, past the phone box across the road, and up the muddy bank and across the field to the edge, which would then allow them to go up the muddy path to the train line, and along to the old guard's hut. They slowed to a stop, and heard a call.

The police meanwhile were driving up and down the main road in their panda cars, trying to keep the local residents calm with their reassuring presence. Local people were ringing the police station and reporting loud bangs and unusual calls and screams but of course the policemen who were doing the regular beats couldn't hear or see anything, so they just kept driving up and down the main road to appease the worried public.

A car hurtled around the corner, and came to a standstill, just opposite Megan and her mother. Patsy was now fully formed as a demon, and a massive one at that, an awesome sight, and not one to be messed with. So too was Megan, albeit a slightly smaller one.

"I see the bitches are here," she quietly sneered to Megan.

"No, Mum, not bitches, witches, and good ones at that." Suddenly there was another call, louder this time, and nearer. "Oh no, it's him," said Megan quite wobbly now at the sight unfurling before her eyes.

"He will not hurt you tonight, I will not let him, and he knows that. We will all have to work together to get this nasty bastard, he's ruining it for us all," she said.

Suddenly and is if on cue, a large pair of green eyes emerged from the darkness, and there he was, that man, bigger now, much bigger, just as Megan remembered him from all those years ago in Ireland in the square opposite the Royal Oak pub; black wings, very long fangs, huge talons, and a massive tail.

"Hello, my beauties." He slithered his eyes all over Megan and licked his lips.

"You touch one hair on her head and I will kill you myself," Megan's mother quietly warned him in a slithering type language, one Megan had not heard before but one she still totally understood somehow.

Megan's stomach lurched and her head spun; she suddenly felt a connection to this massive demon. She could see into his mind, and could tell what he was thinking and how he was feeling and what she felt was lust! It was a feeling she had never felt before and it made her dizzy.

Oh, God, she's connected, Megan's mother thought recognising the signs. "Don't, don't let him in like I did for God's sake," and with that she slapped Megan hard around the head.

"Ow! Mum please don't; everyone's watching," she cried back at her.

"Get him out of your head. Never, ever let him in like I did, do you understand? Never!"

"She just bloody slapped Megan, the mental bitch!" screamed Sally inside the parked car.

"Calm down, Sally, he was trying to connect to Megan and very nearly succeeded," said an exasperated Claire. "It's the only way she knows how to protect her."

"Bloody funny way of protecting someone," replied a very tearful Sally. "You should have seen the bloody bruises on her body when she first came to me then you would all understand," she exclaimed.

"Yes but this is now, and a totally different situation. Now calm down – we have work to do," said Claire.

The three demons stood looking at each other, eyes glowing.

"Can you see it?" asked Megan's mother.

"No, not yet," Megan replied. "Wait! It's coming."

All of the lights on the estate suddenly went out, one by one. They all stood in complete darkness. There wasn't even a star in the night sky; it was as if someone above had just turned all the lights in the world off, it was that dark.

In the distance far down the train line, a pair of bright yellow eyes appeared; 2 little dots at first, but growing larger by the minute.

"He's cloaking," Megan called out. Everyone crouched down as a red mist started to appear above the old abandoned guard's hut. It slowly turned into a red ball with a blue and white edge, which was glowing like a beacon. "That's it," cried Megan.

"He's calling them in," said Sally.

"Bloody hell!" said Claire. "Clever bloody girl, I knew she was a goodun when I first met her."

The ball of light was now getting larger and a terrible screaming sound could be heard emanating from this throbbing window. Several creatures had flown out, and were circling right in front of the parked car where the three girls were. A lovely ginger cat came slinking around the corner, keeping low, and trying to evade the awful sounds in the air. It crept along the hedge next to their parked car, using it for cover, but there was a sudden squeal, and a flurry of wings, and the cat was gone, grabbed by one of the winged creatures, never to be seen again.

"That's it, that's what's killing everything here, it all makes sense now," Claire cried out.

"What does?" asked a still tearful and worried Sally.

"He's a rogue demon. He looks a nasty bastard. They roam from area to area cloaking so no one can see them, living on cats and dogs, sheep, cattle even horses. They drink the blood similar to vampires, but their bodies do not quite work the same, and to progress and carry on they need to feed on a human soul. The blood sustains them. Look at this." She pulled out a wad of police reports, detailing how 5 children, all male, had been reported missing over the last year. "In every event, there were also reports of dead or missing cats, dogs, sheep, cows etc, and it says here the perpetrator was probably a large wolf which had escaped from somewhere. The reason they decided to keep it hush hush, was so as not to frighten the public. The police decided to investigate this under cover, bloody idiots. It's because of that decision that more kids have died, and we are here tonight," cried Claire.

The red portal window was now massive, and everyone who was there could see it clearly. It looked like a massive red cloud edged with glowing fiery gold. It was revolving high in the deep black/indigo sky, with all sorts of weird creatures flying in and out of it, all of them carrying some kind of squealing animal. Without warning, a large screaming dog flew by just missing the roof of the parked red Ford Escort, which Claire, Elaine and Sally were sat in.

They were all watching the carnage unravelling in front of them and were horrified to see that the dog was grasped by a very large and nasty looking beastie which was heading straight for the red oblivion. Then suddenly from nowhere, with a bright flash of lightning, and accompanied by surprised gasps from the three occupants of the car, two Archangels suddenly landed in full view of everyone. They were both enormous, standing at least 8 feet tall, with massive wings that looked as big as those on a glider, which puffed out angel dust, sprinkling everything that surrounded them as they unfolded and shook out their wings after a long journey, which amazed and humbled the worried onlookers. The dust, which has hardly ever been seen by humans was a special sparkling, precious and very rare gift from God. Angel dust sprinkled everywhere as they landed, and then very quickly the wings were retracted back into their bodies for their protection. Angels' wings are very prone to damage when in a fight, and this is something both angels needed to try to avoid, as damage to wings meant months of angel hospital time, which none of them really ever wanted, as it took them out of their role as protectors and leaders of the human race, such is their devotion to us, down here on earth.

"Oh my goodness!" said Megan bowing to them.

They smiled, acknowledged all three demons and bowed back, but didn't say a word.

"Oh!" screamed Elaine. "They have sent in the big boys."

"What did you expect?" replied Claire with a smile on her face. "This is a very serious situation," she added as the rogue demon finally came into view.

You could smell him coming, and a slight breeze brought with it a smell of death. It was a horrible, rotting stench, which made Megan feel very sick. As the demon got nearer, the portal seemed to get even busier.

"They're hunting for food now," said Claire.

Nearer and nearer came the demon, and everyone including the angels was crouched down. It was pitch black, and all that could be seen was a massive red and gold hole in the sky, literally throbbing, with hundreds of winged creatures flooding in and out. The screams of dying animals being devoured filled the air, and now the flashing lights started, almost like disco lights, throbbing to the sound of a rhythm.

"He's here," Megan whispered to her mother.

"We will have to be quick now, once he arrives at the portal, he will close it until tomorrow," she told Megan.

The two Archangels called for the large demon and Megan's mother to follow them. The two Archangels then nodded to one another and the very next moment, the rogue demon came into full view.

This was a large demon, in fact he was massive. His flesh was rotting, and falling off in chunks, which accounted for the smell, and his tail stretched out like a lizard, slapping the ground as he walked along. Big yellow eyes shone like torches. His wings were partially rotted away, but his fangs and talons were much, much bigger than those of the other 2 demons, and disturbingly a line of fire ran down his back, little flames jumping up and out of his dorsal line with every breath he took.

"I wonder what he's been hunting tonight?" said Claire watching everything through a very large pair of binoculars.

You could have cut the air with a knife it felt so thick. The two Archangels crept towards the bottom of the muddy path, signalling to both of the other demons to go either side of them.

Megan's mother turned to her and said, "Stay here."

"Mum!" Megan replied.

"Stay here, this is not your fight," and with that Sally appeared at Megan's side.

"Come on, love, sit this one out, they know what they are doing," and she dragged a very reluctant Megan to join Elaine and Claire, who were now out of the car and standing with binoculars studying the ongoing paranormal event that was unfolding in front of their eyes.

"I've never seen anything like this before," commented Claire.

"Bloody hell, must be a rarity," replied Elaine, both of them talking and watching what was happening, although Claire was the only one with binoculars.

"They are getting ready to attack," whispered Claire. "He's glowing now, getting ready to throw the carcass he's holding, into the portal, and then he'll close it, and go to his lair until the next time it opens. He's feeding them," she said with sheer distain. "Oh, God, no," cried Claire.

"What?" said the other 3 all at the same time and looking at her with worried expressions.

"What?" screamed Megan.

"The carcass," said Claire, "it's human!"

"What!" they all screamed simultaneously.

"Could that be the boy?" asked Claire.

"Let me look," said Megan, tearing the binoculars out of her hands. Physically shaking, she focused on the horrible sight in front of the portal and could see quite clearly the body of Stuart Green, hanging like a rag doll over the shoulder of the demon. Megan immediately dropped the binoculars, and ran over to her mother.

"What the bloody hell did I tell you?" she growled, her eyes the biggest and meanest that Megan had ever seen.

"Mum, he's got Stuart."

"Oh hell!"

Sally suddenly grabbed Megan from behind. "For God's sake, girl, do you want to get yourself killed? Come on and do as your mother told you," and with that she dragged her back to where the others were waiting.

All 3 grabbed the still struggling Megan.

"Stop!" shouted an exasperated Claire. "Leave them to it, you have done your bit, the Archangels didn't come to earth for nothing. I know you want to help, and it will be your turn in years to come, but now, no! Let them deal with this, okay, young lady?"

"Okay," replied a very tearful Megan. "I don't want my mum to be hurt," she cried.

"She won't be. What you think your big bad demon of a mother would let any demon kill her? Come on now, love, I don't think so, you should know better." Megan smiled through her tears and acknowledged their concern. "Now let's watch and see what happens, it will get really nasty."

The two Archangels were now talking to one another telepathically.

"We need to try and get the child away," Metatron said to Demion.

"He's probably dead already," replied Demion.

"No he's not I still sense a light. We must at least try." They nodded to one another as they finalised their attack plan, allowing the demons to hear them.

"They are planning to try and rescue Stuart, but it could be too late," said Megan.

"How the bloody hell do you know that?" asked Claire.

"I can hear them talking," she replied.

The two Archangels moved forward slowly, followed by the two demons.

"What do they have to do?" Claire asked Megan.

"They have to get the demon into the portal, and then they will throw in a shooting star which will implode. Demons can't live in the light, and this will help light up the portal, stunning the demon for a moment, allowing them time to get everything back in and seal up the door."

"Bloody hell, that's going to take some doing," said Claire.

"I know," Megan replied shakily.

The demon was now growling and shaking Stuart like a rag doll.

"Shit, he's still alive," said Claire.

"Oh, God!" cried Megan, big bumbling tears running down her face.

The 3 girls grabbed her.

"You can't do anything, love, this is all part of life," said an also tearful Sally hugging and kissing her.

The demon was trying to revive Stuart, who was now very near death. The demon needed him to be alive when he threw him into the portal so that they could all feed on his soul. This gave the Archangels an opportunity. They had now decided that Stuart couldn't be saved, but with the help of the two demons, one on either side, they could tip the big bugger and Stuart back into the portal.

The demon was now raging with frustration, whacking Stuart harder and harder trying to get some response, but he was dying. The moment came which gave the Archangels an opportunity which they very quickly took advantage of. From seemingly nowhere they suddenly produced the most ornate and antique looking spears. It was as if God had created them himself. The spears suddenly started to glow.

"Now!" Metatron shouted to Demion, and they lunged forward up the bank which still concealed them in the darkness. Just as they reached the top of the bank, both Archangels rammed their spears into the demon at the same time, one at each side.

"Oh they've speared him," cried Claire watching through the binoculars. "Go on get the bastard," she was crying out.

The two demons ran up behind the Archangels in a pincer movement. While the Archangels had the demon skewered, the two demons would move in and lift him back into the portal. The rogue demon let out a terrifying death squeal and the other nasty beasties reacted immediately to his call and came flying out of the portal not really realising what was happening. However, as soon as they saw the Archangels and the two demons, they started their bombarding attack. Every time a beastie hit an Archangel, sparks flew, lighting up the sky like a firework display. The two demons now attacked from the rear, and the beasties charged into them as well, their claws as sharp as Samurai swords, slicing and cutting into the demons, and making them bleed, an action which would eventually start to weaken them.

"Shit!" screamed Claire watching the raging battle through the binoculars.

"What?" called the girls.

"It's getting bloody."

The two Archangels were now under total attack. They had the demon skewered from each side, and they called to the demons to help lift up the bastard demon and push him into the portal, but there were so many of the wicked beasties, that they were draining the demons' energy.

"Come on, one more push," called Metatron, but the skewered demon was calling and screaming even louder, rallying his troops and they were responding, hitting and slicing the 2 demons trying to help their master who was now calling louder and louder.

The beasties somehow sensed that these two were the weak link, so they hit them hard with everything they had. The 2 demons bled, and blood meant weakness, so they concentrated their attack on the demons, who were now bleeding profusely, which was just what they wanted.

The smell of the demons' blood filled the air, sending the winged beasties into even more of a frenzy, who continued to attack, cutting and shredding the 2 demons with all their might.

The Archangels suddenly realised that they were weakening.

Metatron looked across at Demion and said, "Call the girl."

"No, the girl's too young," he replied.

"She's our only hope, call her," he demanded.

Demion telepathically called to Megan, "Help us now."

"No!" screamed Claire when Megan told her what Demion had said. "No, Megan you can't."

But it was too late, she was already gone. Running up the embankment, Megan was shocked at the terrible sight before her. Both Archangels held the skewered demon aloft on their spears, the demon was still holding on to Stuart, who was now just flopping around deader than a rag doll, whilst the two demons, their skin ripped to shreds, were bleeding profusely and were being

147

bombarded by literally hundreds of the bloody beasts. She spied a large branch, thick and heavy just to one side of her, and picked it up. God only knows how, but he must have been helping, and with one big sweep into the sky, she literally knocked 200 of the beasties out of the air, and away from the 2 demons. They both gasped and glanced in Megan's direction as if to say thank you, and then together gave the final push that allowed the Archangels to finally throw the demon into the portal.

"Bloody hell, go, Megan!" screamed Claire in sheer delight.

"What, what?" screamed Elaine and Sally, just as they were all thrown to the ground by a massive explosion that rocked through the air. It was like an atom bomb going off, making the shape of a mushroom as the red coloured smoke and clouds rose high into the dark sky.

The two demons were in a really bad way and the big boy had already left by the time Claire, Elaine and Sally arrived. The two Archangels were talking to Megan, and thanking her for everything.

"But I didn't do anything," she replied.

"You did more than you realise, without you and your mother's help, the rogue would still be here. He's gone now, so thank you," said Demion.

Megan's mother was bleeding, her skin emitting tiny green glistening particles that are present in demon blood.

"She will be fine, but will need a little attending to," said Metatron, as he sprinkled angel dust over her mother, who screamed as the dust bubbled on her skin, emitting a vile smelling vapour.

Suddenly and as if by magic (angel magic) she calmed and the wounds started to close.

"She is very weak, but will survive. We must go now. Until we meet again, young one, something you can be certain of," said Demion. Both the Archangels bowed to Megan, opened their massive wings, which sparkled with tiny golden stars, lifted up and were gone.

"Bloody hell, never, ever thought I would see that," Elaine said as she got a blanket out of the car, and was walking towards Megan's mother.

"Right then," shouted Sally, "me, Claire and Elaine will look after Mum tonight, my young lady, as you will need your sleep. You will have to do everything this weekend. In the car," she ordered.

Megan went to bed that night leaving the 3 witches nursing her mother.

Bloody hell! she thought. *She would kill them if she realised that they were looking after her.*

But the Archangels had said that she was weak and needed looking after, so she went to bed exhausted, prayed and thanked her angels for their protection that night. She prayed too that Stuart had died painlessly, and asked that his spirit might be able to come back and talk to her, and most of all, thanked them for her friends, the 3 witches (Claire, Elaine and Sally).

I don't know at this moment in time, where I would be without them, she thought.

Chapter 26

Nursing Mum

Megan woke Saturday morning realising that she had overslept. It was now 8 in the morning.

Oh, God, Mother will kill me, she thought. She got up and ran into her mother's bedroom. The 3 girls had gone and her mother was sleeping peacefully. Her face was swollen, and was hardly recognisable. Her skin was blackened, and her hands and feet were swollen and sore, but she was alive, and asleep. "Thank God," Megan said out loud and looking up.

Megan ran down the stairs and put the oven on, and quickly made the soda bread, and got it into the oven. Then she suddenly realised that no one was awake.

"Oh goodness, slow down, relax, and stop panicking," she told herself, as she saw a note pinned on the pantry door. It read:

Megan, Mum will be fine, please make some soup for her today. The money for the shopping along with the list is in the cheese dish in the larder. Please make sure Mum has plenty to drink, and don't expect her up until Monday. I'll be around to see you Sunday, love Sally, Elaine and Claire.

"Oh, God thank you," she said silently taking the cheese dish out of the pantry, opening it, and finding a bundle of paper notes inside. There was £25 for that week.

That will be fine, she thought as she read the list before putting it back and looking in the fridge to see what she could do for breakfast.

The local newspaper and television stations announced that day a body had been found. The police had said that the coroner had asked for an autopsy, and that no identification had been made yet, but two police cars now sat outside the Greens' house in the cul-de-sac, and would be there for the next two days.

Megan cooked, washed and cleaned that Saturday, her mother not moving from her bed. She had made her favourite soup, leek and potato, and fed it to her, much to her mother's disgust, while she lay in bed, turning over and not acknowledging her as Megan left the bedroom.

She's getting better, Megan happily thought.

Sally arrived Sunday morning just as Megan had finished washing-up from breakfast.

"Hello, sweetheart," said Sally as she cuddled and kissed her as usual. "Where are the kids?" she asked.

"Out playing," Megan replied.

"How's Mum?" she asked.

"Okay I think. She growled at me this morning when I fed her the soup."

"Oh bloody hell, she's going to give you shit when she's better," Sally laughed.

"No she won't," replied Megan.

"What?" said Sally.

"She won't," Megan repeated. "We had a stand-off."

"What!" cried Sally looking directly into Megan's happy smiling face.

"Yes, I lost it a bit," said Megan.

"But what happened to cause that?" asked Sally, now starting to be upset and very agitated.

"That nasty Father Quinn called round one night demanding money from Mum. She told him Dad was away, and she didn't know where he was which is true we don't and he accused Mum of being a harlot and being paid by other men. He was drunk," said Megan.

"Oh that bloody evil man. Sorry, Megan, but you know how I feel after Harold?"

"Of course I do," she replied, "but I kicked him in the knee after he grabbed Mum."

"Oh sod!" said Sally.

"And he said he would make a complaint to the police that I assaulted him. I told him I would complain to the police that he had assaulted my Mum. He really grabbed her hard by the arm, and harassed her for money. Oh, Sally what have I done?"

"Megan stop, this is one really nasty man, I remember you telling me about him calling for money."

"But there's more," said a now very nervous Megan.

"What?" asked Sally.

"I heard him say he was going to contact the council and have us evicted because we have some rent arrears, and he is going to my headmaster and will talk to Sergeant Brown to help him. So it's his fault that we've been hassled by the council and are now going to be evicted." "Okay right, let me think. First of all, are you okay here: food, cleaning, ironing, washing uniforms, is there anything I can do for you?" she asked.

"No all done," Megan replied.

"Oh goodness, you are a good and very special girl, and I love you so much," she said as she gave her another cuddle.

"And I love you too, Sally, thank you for being in our lives."

"Right, what's for lunch?" Sally asked.

"Slow roast breast of lamb with sage, onion and apricot stuffing (the usual one) but spiked with garlic and rosemary for a change, cauliflower and leek cheese, carrots, cabbage and roasties and minted gravy."

"Oh wonderful," said Sally.

"And apple and raspberry crumble with clotted cream for pudding."

"Oh you are clever," Sally said looking admirably at her. "And supper?"

"Pink salmon sandwiches and crisps."

"Perfect," said Sally smiling.

Chapter 27

Tragedy

Stuart's body was found half a mile from his house, under a hedge, in the bottom horses' field just down from the cul-de-sac. Extra foliage had been placed over him, covering the lair in which he had been placed. He was positioned neatly in the foetal position. His eyes were missing, his skin burned to a crisp, his chest a bloody mass of leaking guts and lungs, and every single drop of blood had been drained from his body. There was also a terrible deep mark gouged out on his back. He was the fifth child to be found that had been killed in a similar way, with the same marks on their backs. The other instances had been reported over the last 2 years by the police in neighbouring counties.

Little Stuart Green was a local boy who lived with his mum and gran, and little sister Shelly. At the age of 11, he did a morning and evening paper round, Monday to Friday for the local newsagent, and sometimes he would work at the local pub, helping them out at the last minute, bottling up if the usual chap didn't show. He was quite small for his age, had dark ginger hair, freckles and a lovely smile, and the biggest light brown eyes you ever saw, which of course, if you didn't know him, made him stand out in the crowd.

He would often be seen carrying shopping for his grandmother who lived with them, and would accompany her to the shops where he would often bump into Megan. They would all chat and laugh and depart, agreeing happily to meet up again in the very near future.

He lived in a terraced house around a cul-de-sac which overlooked a golf course on the edge of the estate, a really nice area, very quiet, and also very clean. The golf course ran adjacent to big connecting fields that were normally full of horses, the fields being full of the most wonderful wild flowers imaginable, which Shelly, his sister, often picked for her mother with pride. This was a very quiet spot, with not much going on, and his mother Shirley Green was a really good mum, a widow, who worked really hard to keep her family clean and fed. She was able to work because her mother Maureen lived with her. Her husband had left just before Shelly was born, and when he died in an accident at work they were separated but not divorced. It was quickly decided that Maureen would move in with them, and help with her grandchildren, whom she adored. It worked, and for years they were a lovely happy unit, all supporting each other in their struggle with day to day life.

They were a good family, tight, loving and well-respected in the local community, and now their little world had fallen apart. All of them were in total shock, and his mother Shirley was now in a never ending tortuous hell, one it seemed she could never escape from!

Chapter 28

The chair

The day of the eviction was drawing near. Megan's mother was cooking late into the night, every night trying to raise extra money from the sales of the pies to the local pubs. They were selling like hot cakes, literally, but the pressure was beginning to tell, and with no word from their father, who they knew was working at Oldbury Power Station, and with no way of even getting there to try and find him, it felt like a lost cause. Patsy had no one to help her except Megan, but she was just a child, a demon child, the thought of which still churned her stomach. She felt like she was drowning, but she just kept baking and baking, trying to blot out the worry of eviction, and the rejection of her beloved husband. She was drinking more which didn't help, falling to bed every night exhausted and very drunk, and it was a miracle that she managed to work at all.

That night Megan closed her bedroom curtains, pushed the bedroom door closed and got into bed and put a pair of earphones into her ears. She pulled the blankets over her head, and switched on her small transistor radio, turning it on to listen to Tony Prince from Radio Luxemburg. Sally had given the radio to her as a present for doing well in her exam.

Bless Sally, Lord, she thought as she snuggled down listening to the Kinks', 'Love is all around'. The demon could howl, the baby could cry, and the noise on the stairs could go on all night, but at last, Megan could sleep better.

The next morning, she had just finished the washing-up, and the tidying when she looked at the clock. Her brothers and sister had already left for school, but she was running a little behind as she was trying to finish preparing the vegetables for tea to help her mother as much as possible. She knew how tired and stressed she would be when she came home from work, so, anything she could do to make life easier was done.

There was suddenly an unexpected knock at the front door. She was trying to wipe her hands and get to the door as quickly as she could, when the door knocked again, really hard and loud this time. Her stomach told her this was trouble.

"Coming," she called out really loud before opening the door slightly and peering out. There at the front door was the rent officer Nigel Dickenson, and Sergeant Brown.

"May we come in?" Nigel Dickenson asked.

"No," replied Megan emphatically.

"Where's your mother?" he then asked.

"At work, why?" she asked him.

"Any sign of the rent arrears being paid?"

"Don't know you will have to ask Mum."

Mr Dickenson handed her a letter.

"You have until 12 o'clock midday Saturday to pay the arrears or the sergeant and his men will evict you," said Mr Dickenson.

"Yes we bloody will," retorted Sergeant Brown snarling and curling his lip excitedly. He rubbed his hands together and glared at her like a hungry dog. "I can't wait to rid the community of you bloody Murphy troublemakers."

"Now, now," said Mr Dickenson glaring back at Sergeant Brown. "Sorry, but it's 12 midday, Saturday." He turned and pulled the protesting sergeant down the garden path.

She slammed the door shut so hard, it banged like a clap of thunder.

"Pigs!" she screamed at the inside of the door. "Oh, God and angels we really need your help, and we need it now. Please! Thank you!" she called out loud and looking up. She quickly left for school realising she would be late. "Oh crap, I'll have to run all the way now," and she did.

School seemed to drag. All she wanted to do that day was to go home and make sure that her mum was okay, but someone or something was continually talking to her in her head, but all she could make out was the word 'chair'. In fact it nearly drove her crazy, constantly looking around all the time to try and pick up who was trying to talk to her, but she could see nothing, just the continual word 'chair'. She decided to ring Sally on the way home.

"Hello," came the voice of Sally.

"Sally it's me."

"Hello, my darling, how are you?" came the reply.

"Sergeant Brown and the rent officer knocked on the door at 8.30 this morning. If the rent isn't paid by 12 midday tomorrow we are out, and Sergeant Brown said he couldn't wait to get rid of us."

"Fucking bastard. Evil shit!" she screamed down the phone. "Bloody harassment, that's what it is. Sorry, darling please don't worry."

"I am trying not to, but all I keep hearing is the word 'chair', it's driving me crazy."

"Okay, it must mean something. Think and think hard, is there a chair somewhere that could mean something?"

"Why yes, it's the old boy's chair. Mum wouldn't let us burn it; she loves it, and is going to recover it. Oh, Sally she is cooking all night for the local pubs, she's exhausted."

"Right then, lass, bring the chair into the kitchen, and give your mother a little comfort. I'll drop round a throw and a couple of nice cushions for it. It may at least give her somewhere nice to sit instead of that bloody horrible old stool," she replied.

"Oh, Sally thank you."

"My pleasure, my darling, and please don't worry, my guides keep telling me all will be well."

"Thank you and God bless." Megan put the phone down, got out of the phone box and started to run home.

Outside the front door in a carrier bag was a lovely caramel coloured throw and two matching caramel and chocolate cushions.

"Oh they match the chair," Megan said to herself as she ran through the alley to the backdoor and let herself into the kitchen with the spare key hidden in the dog kennel. She peeled back the tarpaulin; the chair sparkled. *Lovely and comfy*, she thought. *Mum must be out; she is probably down the shop or the off license.*

It was Friday night, fish and chip night. She ran upstairs and changed, putting all her school clothes in the laundry bin for washing the next day, trying at the same time to put out of her mind the fact that they could probably be evicted at midday, but Sally kept telling her that everything would be fine, and she believed her. Suddenly Michael appeared in front of her.

"Oh, hello," she said to him, "thank you for coming, are we being evicted tomorrow?" she asked.

He looked at her and smiled. "All will be well, child."

Oh bloody God, sometimes they get on my bloody nerves talking in riddles all the time, she thought.

"Trust!" said Michael louder and firmly.

"Oh sorry, yes of course," she replied tearfully before running to the kitchen.

She uncovered the chair, and pulled it to one side, then went into the kitchen and picked up the old rickety stool that had seen its day, and took it outside. She then picked up the armchair and dragged it into the kitchen, clumsily tearing the back panel.

"Oh feck!" she cried to herself putting the chair into the corner of the kitchen where the stool had been. She put the cream throw over the chair and added the cushions. *There, that will do her good*, she thought.

Her brothers and sister came in screaming and laughing.

"What's for tea?" they all asked at once hungrily.

"Fish and chips, dummies, it's Friday!"

"Hooray!" they all shouted at once and ran upstairs to change.

Megan finished her usual Friday chores and was just laying the table when her mother came through the front door. She walked straight into the kitchen, saw the chair, put down her bags of shopping and burst into tears. This was the first time that Megan had ever seen her mother cry. Her brothers and sister ran into the kitchen, spilling toast crumbs from the tea and toast Megan had made them while they were changing.

"What's wrong, Mum?" they all asked looking very concerned.

"I have just come from the rent officer; the pubs paid me £40 today for the pies, so I went and paid it straight off the rent arrears. We still owe £160, and I have only got until midday tomorrow and unless a bloody miracle happens..."

Megan cut her off. "Right you three you can go and get the fish and chips tonight," and with that she gave them a five pound note and the shopping bag. "Go on now, see you in about 10 minutes," she said and pushed them out of the door. They happily ran down the street, screaming and shouting to one another, happy to be getting their usual Friday fish and chips. "I'll go to the off license for you," she said turning to face her mother.

"Thank you for the chair. I bought some material today, it's cream. How did you guess the colour?" she asked.

"Sorry to tell you, but the back panel split as I picked it up."

"Oh let me look," her mother said pulling the chair away from the corner so she could look at it. "Oh that's not too bad. I'll pull that off. I have enough to cover that," and with that she pulled the whole panel of ripped fabric off the back of the chair, and they both stood speechless, looking at each other with tears in their eyes. Then Megan's mother started crying again, because right there looking straight at them were bundles and bundles of money: £5 pound notes, 10 shilling notes and most of all £20 notes.

158

"Oh thank you, angels. That's why we were not meant to burn that chair," said Megan. They quickly counted all the money and put it on the table; it totalled £390.10 shillings. "Just think, Mum, if this had gone to the bonfire, it would have all gone up in smoke, and no one would have been any the wiser."

"I will be outside that rent office at 9 in the morning, when they open, to pay the arrears off, and pay advance rent," she replied to Megan. For once her mother actually spoke nicely to her, and it gave Megan a warm feeling inside. Perhaps at last her mother was beginning to love her. Only time would tell. "Right, you mustn't say anything to anyone. Anyone!" she growled at Megan.

"I won't, Mum," she replied.

"Right, large tonight," and she put a ten shilling note in her hand and a note, and almost, almost, smiled at Megan.

Megan hopped and skipped all the way down to the off license, and passed the note and the 10 shillings over to the barmaid.

"You look happy today," said the barmaid.

"Thank you," Megan replied.

"Any good luck stories to tell?" the barmaid asked as she passed over the large bottle of sherry.

"Nah, just been a nice day," Megan replied.

"Well don't drink it all at once," the barmaid laughed to her as she left through the door.

"I won't," called back Megan, as she ran up the road to her house.

That night's fish and chips were the best ever: mushy peas with a tad of vinegar, salt and pepper and a dot of butter all added to the taste, and spirits were high. Their mother actually sat at the table with them to eat. A big pot of tea soon emptied, and after all the bread and butter had been eaten, and bellies were full, their mother said, "Early to bed tonight please, it's going to be a busy day tomorrow, and maybe, if everything pans out okay, we'll go to the zoo on Sunday." Screams of delight filled the air. "I'll wash up." She turned to face Megan. "Listen, I have got to get back here by 12 o'clock with the receipt, so I will be gone early, so don't open the door, whatever you do, don't let them in until I get home, understand?"

"I do," Megan replied and then ran upstairs with her brothers and sister. Michael suddenly appeared. "Thank you, Michael," she called out to him.

"Child it will be difficult tomorrow, but all will be well in the end."

"Thank you," she called back.

"We are watching."

"I know you are," and with that he vanished.

She closed the curtains waving goodnight out of the window, jumped into bed and said her prayers before switching on her transistor radio, putting in her earphones, and gently falling asleep.

Chapter 29

Eviction day

Saturday morning was really like every other Saturday. Megan was up early, made soda bread, and cooked breakfast for everyone. Today it was eggs, streaky bacon, sausages, tomatoes from the garden grilled with salt and pepper and a dot of butter on the top which made them bubble and crisp, and a tin of button mushrooms which were again pan fried with salt and pepper with a dot of butter. It was all served with some quickly made bubble and squeak from the leftover cold veg from the meals in the week. It never lasted long.

Then the beds were stripped and freshly remade, the bedrooms, bathroom and toilet all cleaned and tidied, and the red tiles in the hallway polished. These were the usual Saturday chores. Megan seemed to have it all done quickly that day, and had already put the bed linen into the beloved twin tub and was now preparing lunch, which was broccoli and cauliflower soup with toasted ham and cheese sandwiches.

Megan was just popping a chicken stock cube into the bubbling saucepan containing the cauliflower, broccoli, onions and potatoes, when there was a knock at the door. Her brothers and sister were playing upstairs in their bedrooms, and had been ordered to stay there until their mother came home. She nervously looked at the clock on the kitchen wall, and saw that it was 10.30. The door knocked again and Michael appeared at her side.

"Keep your nerve, child," he said to her, "12 o'clock is the deadline."

She walked to the front door, and then went into the front room and looked out of the large window.

"Open the door, you rug rats!" screamed Sergeant Brown.

"Stop it," screamed Nigel Dickenson. "Hello, Megan where's Mum?" he asked.

"Out," she replied. "She will be back by 12 o'clock."

"I want you out now!" hollered Sergeant Brown at the top of his voice.

"If you don't shut up, I will bloody well remove you myself, do you understand, William?"

"All right, all right, but get it over with," Sergeant Brown screamed back, stomping out of the garden gate and heading towards his parked police car.

Outside there was a string of police cars, 3 council vans and a large removal van.

Oh, God, they really are trying to get rid of us, Megan thought nervously. Neighbours had started gathering outside, all discussing the escalating situation.

"Megan are you sure she will be back for 12 o'clock?" Nigel Dickenson asked again through the window a little later on, nervously glancing at his watch. It was now 10 past 11, 50 minutes to go, but there was still no sign of her mother. A red Ford Escort with racy wheels slowly passed the house, taking in the scene, and eventually parking further down the road.

Megan's brothers and sister were by now very upset, and none of them were allowed out of the house. There was also no sign of their mother, and police and council officials stood outside the house in the street watching every possible movement that might be made by any of the intended evictees. Megan had locked the gate to the back garden really well. Her father had made it, and had triple bolted it, and the bow of the plum tree over the top of the gate made it almost impossible to get in. She heard the gate rattle and checked all the downstairs windows and doors, running from room to room. They were trying to intimidate her. There was still no sign of her mother, and it was now 11.45.

"Oh, God come on, Nigel, the bitch is not going to show up, break the bloody door down, and let's get this bunch of trash out," Sergeant Brown screamed loudly so everyone could hear.

"If you touch that door 1 minute too early, you can kiss goodbye to any eviction, it has to be done by the book. Now, Sergeant," said a very harassed and shaky Nigel Dickenson pointing at Sergeant Brown, "piss off and get back into your bloody car." Nigel once again called to Megan. "Are you sure that your mother is coming back?"

"Yes," screamed Megan, "she will be here," and then another car pulled up outside, and out stepped social worker Angie Wells.

"Don't harass the children, Nigel. Everyone get away from the house until 12 o'clock. All of you! Piss off and get out of the garden," she ordered the loitering policemen at the top of her voice and pointing to the road.

"Oh, Mum please hurry," called Megan, now very distressed and crying. It was now 11.58.

The street was now filled with onlookers, police, council officials and now social workers and a very large well-built man stood at the gate with a brand new, shiny sledgehammer in his hands, and an even bigger grin on his face. Reggie Wallis was the local thug, who made his living working for the local bailiffs. He loved smashing down doors, and delighted in causing misery and distress for folks. He had served 10 years in the nick for doing just that, but now was his chance to return the favour, and being paid for it turned him on even more. He was eyeing up the smartly painted bright yellow door, and admiring how the brass knocker and hinges gleamed in the sunshine.

"Twelve o'clock!" screamed Sergeant Brown.

Nigel looked across at Angie Wells and nodded. "Okay, Reggie," he called out, "all yours."

Reggie's eyes lit up, and he was now ready to smash the door into smithereens, he walked up to the gate to open it, but although it rattled, it wouldn't move. With a very big erection poking out of his jeans in view of everyone, he started attacking the gate, but it just did not open. It was as if some magical force was holding the gate shut, not allowing Reggie in at all, Nigel Dickenson and the Sargent had already walked to the front door just some minutes ago, talking to Megan through the letterbox, but now the gate was shut fast and firm, making everyone quite spooked and very worried at the unfolding scene!

"Climb over, you bloody moron!" screamed Sergeant Brown.

Reggie was by now foaming at the mouth. No one else by law could bash down the door, so again and again he hammered the gate with his shiny sledgehammer, getting madder and madder, roaring like a lion in distress. Finally it crumpled.

"At last!" screamed Sergeant Brown running over to the house from his car.

Reggie was now sweating profusely, wide-eyed, almost as if he was totally high on something. Onlookers started to walk away in disgust. No one ever wanted eviction, and never this way. Pulling their children away from the scene, and saying amongst themselves how glad they were it wasn't them in that position, the crowd started to disperse.

Reggie slowly raised the massive sledgehammer ready to strike the blow that would shatter the door into matchwood, and allow the eviction to begin.

This was always his favourite part. He would probably come in his pants it turned him on so much. He adjusted his focus and was getting ready to strike when, "Stop!" screamed a voice. "Stop!" it screamed again. Everyone froze, even Reggie. Do it do it!

The sergeant bellowed at the top of his voice from across the street.

"Stop!" shouted Nigel. "What now?" he shouted at the woman across the road, as Megan's mother came running up the road. She had a brown envelope in her hand marked 'RENT OFFICE'.

"Sorry I'm late, Mr Dickenson, you had an electricity failure this morning at your rent office, and instead of opening at 9 it didn't open until 10." She handed him the brown envelope, and he opened it and read the contents.

"Okay, everyone, the eviction is cancelled," he called.

Sergeant Brown was by now absolutely out of control, screaming, swearing and waving his arms around. "Nigel you weak piece of shit, why did you let the bitch off?" he bellowed. He was quite breathless, extremely agitated and very animated at the ongoing events.

"Simple," Nigel replied, "at 10.02 this morning, she paid off the £160 rent arrears and paid £200 rent in full upfront for another year. She complied with the proposed eviction order, and there is nothing you can do about it, nothing at all, so don't even try. Behave yourself and stop attracting unwanted interest."

"You little whipper snapper, I'll get you thrown out of the Masonic Lodge in disgrace!" hissed Sergeant Brown.

"I don't think so," he replied very calmly, but nervously shaking inside, "I've got too much on you. I've placed it all around, 8 or 9 places in fact, so even if you were to kill me, I'd get you from my grave." He turned and walked away, and down the little hill to his car. It wasn't until he sat in his car that he realised that he had shit himself. *Oh, God, I'm getting out of this,* he thought as he drove away not looking back, and contemplating his future.

Reggie Wallis was in a right state as he was dragged away by his boss like a ferocious bulldog on a lead. He was bundled into an unmarked white transit van owned by Dogs Bollocks Bailiffs, which then sped off down the road at a rate of knots.

"Don't fret, Reg," said David Hall his boss, "I've got another job lined up for you. Harry," he then called to the van driver, "got any clean jeans and boxers for our Reg here?"

"Coming up, Gov," replied the driver.

Hopefully not again, David thought as he took the clothes from the driver and passed them to a very animated Reggie.

The family were all reunited inside the house, and were all hugging each other. Their mother was actually sat in her comfy chair in the kitchen when there was a knock at the door. Megan opened the door, and there stood Angie Wells.

"Just making sure you are all okay," she said, looking at a very happy family scene.

Megan's mother got up out of her chair and walked to the front door. "Why?" she asked. "What the bloody hell would you have done today to help us if I hadn't paid the rent?"

"Well," she replied, "I was only alerted to the problem yesterday. You should have contacted me."

"Piss off," screamed Megan's mother. "You were ready to once again break up my family, so you can all just piss off," she screamed at her, "and leave us alone," and with that she slammed the bright yellow door shut.

Angie Wells stood there, tears in her eyes realising for once Patsy was absolutely right.

Chapter 30

Claire Branning

Sergeant Brown was still screaming at his sidekick, PC Flower. Everyone else had dispersed.

"Sergeant William Brown."

He stopped instantly, turning around and looking at this tall, immaculately dressed lady, with short red hair and big white glasses.

"Yes?" he replied.

"I'd like a word."

"And who the bloody hell are you? Can't you see we are just regrouping from a crappy situation?" he spat at her and turned back to PC Flower. "Get the bloody paperwork done and a report on my desk."

The lady again interrupted before he could finish bellowing his orders, much to the relief of PC Flower. "Sergeant William Brown," she said again in a louder and more assertive voice.

"What?" he screamed back at her, spittle flying out of his enraged mouth and hitting her in the face.

"I am Claire Branning, Special Operations and Internal Affairs of Southward Police Southwest."

At that very moment, Sergeant Brown stopped, looked directly at her and didn't know whether to be sick or have a bowel movement.

"Yes," he meekly replied.

"Come to my car please, I would like to have a word with you."

She turned and walked towards her red Ford Escort, Sergeant Brown following, sweating, gulping and farting in fear all at the same time.

"Not you!" he screamed at PC Flower who was following him like a meek little puppy.

PC Flower said nothing, put his head down, turned around and walked back to the patrol car.

Claire Branning was 45, single and a very secretive person. Born in

Somerset in a small village called Glastonbury, her mother was a practising White Witch, and her father a Warlock. Claire was born into a family of witchcraft and spells, frogs, toads and seasons; everything in their lives revolved around the seasons. Her mother and father were very well known in the world of witchcraft and they travelled the globe, attending seminars and meetings, speaking about the craft, and taking Claire along to witness everything. At a very early age she learned how to disappear (it's actually called cloaking) making her a very unusual person. It was a very hard spell for most witches and warlocks in the higher echelon to do, and do well, but she learned quickly, and found spells easy and could move in and out of our world zone into the next with ease. By the tender age of 15, she was one of the most powerful White Witches known alive. Her powers and spells were quite amazing, and she could also converse and work alongside angels, often travelling up to the higher planes, which eluded most spiritual people. It made them all green with envy.

She was sent to private school, 8 in fact and was practically expelled from them all, until they found St Bart's in Hampshire. Here she met others like her, but none of them were anywhere near as powerful as her, and this made her settle, and get down to work. She eventually left 6 years later with 12 O levels, and 10 A levels, a monstrous feat which made her parents really proud.

She started her working life as a 999 telephone support officer for the police when she was 19 and the work so intrigued her that she decided to become a policewoman. She was eventually accepted into the force and passed her training with ease to become a PC on the beat. After a further 6 years, she took her sergeant's exam, and passed, then studied for her detective's exam, which again she passed with ease. She was also riot trained, and firearm trained, and worked alongside some of the toughest, nastiest policemen you could imagine. Dirty work makes dirty, nasty men, she always told herself.

Often lonely because of her work, and who she was, she never felt the want for a man, whereas women made her feel at ease. She could converse with them, hold a real conversation, and understand what they were thinking, something she could never do with the opposite sex.

She met the love of her life when she was called to an incident at the local council housing offices one day. There, a young man who was so desperate and upset because he had been made homeless, had no job, a baby to support and desperately needed a home to live in was pointing a gun at the woman who was sat on the housing information desk, threatening to blow her head off if she didn't give him a council house. The police were called, and Claire being firearm trained was called in to deal with the situation. It would have almost been love at first sight if she didn't have to concentrate on this poor dick waving a small hand pistol around. She could see the woman was very frightened, her face told the whole story, and her aura was changing violently: greens, blues, and reds. It was very hard for her to concentrate, but relief was felt all round when 2 burly officers manhandled the young man to the ground, and knocked the gun away.

"You okay?" Claire asked her. Her name was Elaine.

"I am now thank you."

"No problem, all in a day's work," replied Claire.

Their eyes met, and later that day they were sat in the local pub sipping Vodkas and slim tonic, passing the time away as if they were old friends. They connected instantly and became close very quickly, both understanding each other and their special skills. They decided not to live together for the moment, but spoke every day, seeing each other every weekend. It made their bond stronger in every way, just the way they both liked it: freedom, need and very much devotion.

It was Elaine who pushed Claire in the direction of undercover, Special Operations. The detective side was fine, but very much pen pushing. She wanted action, adventure, and even more than that, she wanted to get the really bad bastards, who were killing the heart of communities all over the country: paedophiles, drug barons, money launderers, and human traffickers. That was what she had been put on this earth to do.

Her mother had always told her that she would be different, and she was right. She mixed high in the spiritual world, dealt with demons and bad spirits, could sense a vamp or shifter almost half a mile away and woe betide any bad bastard human she pursued, because when she finally got her teeth into them, they wished they had never met her. Yes her spiritual side served her very well in her police work, and it made her a very daunting investigator.

She lived in a quiet unnoticed underground world. Not wishing to be noticed by anyone, she deliberately didn't have a credit card, or any credit accounts, so that it was really difficult for anyone to trace her, or check her out. The police had given her a false identity which she lived under, and it suited her fine; only those very, very close to her knew anything about her, and that was fine for her and fine for the police. It meant that she could investigate most people and groups without anyone realising exactly who she was.

One of her pet hates was paedophilia. She had come across so many traumatized families and children, both boys and girls whose lives had been terribly scarred forever, and parents who were so grief stricken that someone had touched and defiled their precious son or daughter. Revenge was something that the police forbid, however tempting it was. Instead people like Claire were encouraged to get the bastards the proper way, put them in jail, and let them suffer at the hands of the other inmates. Some 90% of jailbirds hated kiddy fiddlers (as they were known inside) and the other 10% spent the whole of their jail term living in fear. Good, give the bastards some of the fear they instilled in the children they abused, was how she looked at it. Taking some of your own medicine was a good tonic, but in Claire's mind, once a paedo, always a paedo and she hated them all, and made a vow to catch every fucker she could and make them pay. Properly of course.

She had been assigned to one particular case which would taste nasty in every policeman's mouth: investigating one of your own. When you become a police officer you take a vow, just like the vow that you take when you marry someone, and you marry yourself to the police. You vow to become one of them, the elite of the protectors, to help and assist all citizens to the best of your ability, to be fair and honest, never to take sides, be the law, and make sure justice prevails.

She did realise, however, that the police at times were a law unto themselves. Every officer was open to a bribe. Cons tried it on. Some took, some didn't, and it was her job to suss out the ones that did. It was also a very backstabbing environment. The police were always encouraged to report on their own, sometimes resulting in difficult moments, like the one that stuck in her brain. She had been passed an anonymous letter saying that one of the beat policemen had bought a very expensive new car, and moved from a tiny 3 bed terraced to a beautiful 5 bed detached house in the leafy suburbs of Nailsea. How could a newly married beat police officer, married to a part time hairdresser afford that? Alarm bells rang and a full investigation pursued, only to find out in the end that they had won half a million pounds on Littlewoods pools the lucky beggars, and had wanted to keep it quiet from everyone! All in a day's work Claire reminded herself.

The Masonic Order was as old as time itself, very secretive, hush hush, and very hard to get into. Very little is known about them, apart from the fact that they look after each other and support charity a great deal, which in itself is quite fantastic. Quite a few very high ranking police officers were well known members of the Masonic Order, which again in itself is not a problem, but could be if a rogue officer, unbeknown to the Order, used it as a screen to cover his tracks. Over the last 3 years, secret notes concerning one particular officer had appeared in her pigeon hole, and each time she investigated, it drew a blank. Still Claire felt the net was slowly closing in on them. The death of a totally unknown paedophile who was a foster parent, for God's sake, had opened a totally new line of enquiry, leading to another arrest, that of a very well-known local headmaster. Yes she was definitely on the trail she realised and it might take time, but unravel it she would.

Sergeant Brown was a constant worry to her. Promoted from the next local county of Devon, he came with a bad reputation, which was quite quickly confirmed by all. He was a bully, and his officers suffered under his command. He enjoyed 2 or 3 Caribbean holidays a year and there were new cars for him and his wife. He also had a very large and expanding pension pot, which was topped up every three months, which did not coincide with his pay. Alarm bells were ringing in Claire's head but still she couldn't put her finger on it.

His wife was a housewife. Louise Brown headed the local W.I. who paid her expenses to run the local branch every month. This was topped up by the regular cheque payments into her savings account of around one hundred and twenty pounds from Henlade School. Once again Claire drew a blank, and it irked her that she just couldn't put her finger on the whole situation, but her gut feeling told her that she was on the right track, she just had to find proof of wrong doing or malpractice. She then decided to ring Ed Scott, the headmaster at the school who paid her, to find out what the payment was in respect of.

She met Ed Scott at a cheese and wine party at the local council offices when the local elections were on 2 years ago. He'd taken a shine to this very tall, sexy, red headed Janet Porter lookalike, and they had got on like a house on fire. When they parted that evening both vowed to each other to keep in touch, but with her work and his demanding wife, they never did.

"Miss Branning," exclaimed a very excited Ed, "how absolutely delicious to see you again," he declared, suddenly embracing her in front of the office staff. "Do come in. Judith, some coffees please," he excitedly screeched across to his secretary, "with biscuits, chocolate!"

"Yes coming," she screeched exasperatedly back. *Oh, God, another bloody funny day with Ed*, she thought to herself.

"Ed," said Claire, "how the hell are you?"

"All the better for seeing you." He gave a wickedly sexy grin, just as Judith knocked on the door and entered without being asked to, with a tray of steaming coffee and chocolate digestives.

"Ed, can you help me?" Claire asked.

"If I can," he replied.

"What can you tell me about Louise Brown?"

"Oh, God!" he replied. "Confidential?" he asked.

"Of course, I give you my word. Can I tell you why I am here?"

"Please," said Ed, and Claire began telling Ed everything. She left 4 hours later, and all the staff had already left the school. Ed was left with only the caretaker to lock up.

Ed really was the only man that had ever actually interested Claire and it was a shame that he was married, but she had Elaine, her lovely stable, reliable, sexy Elaine. No, she would not change her for anything, and she suddenly felt all revved up at the thought of being with her that night.

I'll call in the off license and get a lovely bottle of red wine, she thought to herself as she drove down the school driveway. *Oh, God!* she suddenly thought, *it's the eviction tomorrow; I must ring Sally*, and sped down the road towards home, ready to get all the paperwork together to be at the eviction the next day. She suddenly felt sick, thinking about little Megan and her family.

Sergeant Brown nervously followed Claire to the bright red Ford Escort. He was ushered in to sit in the front seat, and sat there sweating, dabbing his brow with a checkered handkerchief, while Claire sorted paperwork without saying a word, and not even looking at him.

"William, may I call you William?" Claire asked Sergeant Brown.

"Yes," he replied croakily.

"That was a bit over the top don't you think?" she said quietly.

"It's my job to get rid of the scum of the earth, chuck them out, move them on, and that family is nothing but trouble!" he replied back starting to raise his voice.

"Yes, and it is my job to investigate scum of the earth policemen and women who abuse their positions to unlawfully gain money, without paying taxes," she replied looking down at her paperwork, and not at him.

"Are you accusing me of something?" he asked raising his voice even higher.

"No of course not, but it has been brought to my attention that Mrs Brown has been fired as head examiner for Henlade Home Economics Department, for fraudulently claiming expenses."

His face went puce, and his blood drained into his boots.

"What!" he screamed so loud, it nearly burst Claire's eardrums.

"Yes apparently she had claimed for a local hotel room and evening meal for the last 3 years, when in fact she had actually never stayed there; doesn't look good for you does it? Of course I have persuaded the headmaster not to take any action against her, as we don't want the papers to get hold of it, or any black marks to blot your shiny clean record do we now?"

"I really have no idea what you are talking about, young lady. I'd be very careful what you say to me, or I will have a solicitor sort you out, and have you for harassment," he replied sneering at her.

"Well it's a wonder that the Murphys haven't already done that to you, you really are a nasty, vindictive man, Sergeant Brown, and I will be keeping my eye on you. If your wife can get away with embezzlement, how do I know that you are not up to anything? After all, you are family. That will be all, Sergeant Brown," she said closing her file.

"That's all! That's all!" he again bawled back at her, this time right up to her nose, almost touching it, and spraying her once again with spume from his mouth.

"Yes for now," she replied.

"I will have a solicitor on you first thing in the morning," he again bellowed while getting out of the car.

Well, she thought, *why do you need a solicitor if you have nothing to hide?* as she drove down the road on her way to meet up with Elaine.

Chapter 31

The letters

Patsy sat in her comfy chair in the kitchen, with her cup of something in her hand. All the children were in bed asleep, and all was quiet, for now anyway. Somewhere in the distance a dog could be heard howling.

She fingered the crumpled letters she had been fearfully hiding for such a long time, tears trickling down the side of her face. She was regretting not telling someone earlier, as perhaps they could have helped her, but she realised that in reality, she never could have divulged her secret. It was too late now anyway, it was settled. The whole untidy mess had finally come to an end. At least she hoped it had and she quietly prayed that was the case, and that no one could suck any money out of her again.

A dinner plate was placed on top of the stove. Patsy put the papers onto the plate and struck a match, and then sat there watching as the flames engulfed the papers, inhaling the fumes they emitted. Shadows danced across her face as she stared deeply into the orange and yellow flames which reflected in her deep green eyes.

"No need to worry about you Sergeant William Brown, Father Quinn, and especially you Arthur, no more rent money for you, I know you are coming, mum told me, and I will sort you out this time, but this time it will be once and for all, I'll never let you hurt me or my family ever again, ever!! well, at least for the moment," she said to herself quietly, sipping sherry from her cup, and feeling the warm liquid burn as she swallowed.

She felt a hand on her shoulder, and knew that her mother was with her. A feeling of relief engulfed her, and a smile broke out on her tired and worn face, but regret was lingering in her mind. Regret of having to pay that nasty man who had threatened to reveal her to everyone, and took hundreds and hundreds of pounds from her for the privilege of his silence. He had taken food from her children's mouths, and put her into debt and nearly cost her the house. But now that was gone, she could breathe again.

She smiled, raised her cup up to the ceiling and said, "Thanks, Mum," and taking a large gulp, she swallowed. She would sleep well tonight. "Things are going to get better, Mum, I know it, and the Lord knows it. It will won't it?" she asked out loud in a desperate voice, praying at the same time.

The trouble was there was no response!

Chapter 32

Police statement – Stuart Green

How insensitive, thought Sally as she read the police statement in the local paper regarding the death of Stuart Green.

It was put out in print the same day as his funeral and stated that they were sure that Stuart was the victim of a wolf attack, which had also probably been responsible for the death of 5 other children over the last 5 years. There was a similarity in each case, and all the victims had sustained the same injuries, making a wolf attack the most probable explanation.

It was reported that a large wolf which had been worrying his sheep, was shot dead by a farmer 8 miles away. They assumed that this was the wolf responsible for the killings, and now the case would be closed with no further action taken.

What they didn't tell anyone was that the autopsy had confirmed that Stuart had only actually died some 12 hours before his body was found.

Stuart's funeral was a very sad affair, and only 10 people attended. It was a pauper's funeral. Being a single parent, Stuart's mother had virtually no money to bury her beloved son. There was no insurance on his or any of the family's lives, so the social security had to help with the costs. The only flowers on the coffin were a bunch of wild flowers picked from the field opposite where Stuart used to play when he was small.

A large black car took them to the crematorium on the outskirts of the town, but it would be a bus ride back. No one spoke and no one sang the single hymn that the vicar had chosen, as Shirley his mother had been in shock since Stuart's death, and was hardly able to get through a day without crumbling into a tearful heap. Her doctor was very worried about her. She had quit her job, struggled to eat and found it hard to even wash herself. Losing a child must be the hardest thing in the world, especially when your child died painfully; a pain a mother takes on herself and beats herself with every waking moment.

Stuart's family was now shattered, with grief swallowing their whole life and reason for existence. Six months after Stuart died his remaining family perished in a fire at their house. It had started downstairs in the living room, engulfing the whole bottom of the house within minutes. The firemen found Stuart's mother, little sister Shelly and their gran all huddled together in bed in the main bedroom. Apparently the fire had been started deliberately, but only God would ever know that!

Chapter 33

All's well that ends well – or is it?

The family had a wonderful day at the zoo, and screams of delight and laughter filled the air while the children were watching the frolicking penguins performing their aquatic aerobics. Next came the giraffes, lions, white tigers, and elephants; oh goodness, their heads were spinning that day. They chomped on Cornish pasties, and fresh egg mayonnaise sandwiches which their mother had made, lemonade and as many ice creams as they wanted. The sun shone and the children played on the grassy square reserved for picnickers in the zoo.

Patsy sat and marvelled at her wonderful children. She really was proud of them all, especially the two boys. They would have jobs of high standing, perhaps doctors, dentists, or maybe even lawyers. Yes they would do well.

Little Trixie, she'd be fine.

She was a tough little beggar, a survivor, and she would have to be, but she would make it, she knew it.

But Megan, Patsy suddenly came alive thinking to herself, *that bloody demon ruins everything. She's bright and has the gift, but it always brings trouble. Everyone knows, anyone with the gift, always meant trouble.*

"Okay, last time around and then home time," she called out to them.

They packed up their picnic hamper, disposed of all the rubbish and started to make their way around the zoo for the final time, but as they did, Patsy suddenly sensed and heard something. She stopped and looked around, and the hairs started rising on the back of her neck, making her golden bumps start to rise. Behind her she suddenly glimpsed a large pair of yellow/green eyes. Megan also stopped and looked.

"Come on you lot," their mother called out to them, making them walk faster. *Better make this quick*, she thought, and they did, and went straight out of the zoo exit to find the number 9 bus at the bus stop. They boarded it and made their way home feeling very happy and contented.

***

Louise Brown was still crying as she gathered her luggage together at the front entrance to their house.

"William, please, I'm so sorry, I thought I was helping. I don't know what came over me. As soon as I realised it was that Murphy girl, I thought I was doing you a favour," she cried pitifully.

"You silly cow! You could have ruined everything, bringing attention to me and my little business," he exclaimed. "You still want your own car, housekeeper, and bloody Caribbean holidays don't you? What the bloody hell did you think you were doing, you greedy cow? That's what you are, a bloody greedy, spoilt, lazy cow. Now piss off to your mother's for at least 6 months to let things settle. I'll tell everyone your mother is ill, and you are looking after her, this will give time for everything to go quiet."

"Yes, yes of course." She was drowning in tears.

"Right then, bugger off," he demanded pointing to the car outside.

She opened the door and walked to her gleaming new Mercedes Benz car to load her luggage. "You nasty vile man," she whispered under her breath, and then she got mad, threw the rest of her luggage into the boot, got in the car, and drove off.

It would be a 4 hour drive to Colchester where her mother lived in a very nice 5 bedroomed house, on the edge of a national park with beautiful views, and with easy train access to London.

This drive would give her time to think. She knew that her marriage to William was over. She hated the nasty, evil bastard anyway and they never had sex anymore.

She had taken 2 or 3 lovers she could go to anytime for sex, and she was just a little trinket on his arm, she had always known that. He used her to gain attention and to further his career, and all he wanted to do was be a godfather in his own sense, literally, and yes a nasty one!

"Goddam bastard!" she screamed out loud as she was driving. It was time to get even, and yes she would get even. She knew where all his accounts were, his private stashes of money, gold and even the handguns which he thought she knew nothing about. She also knew where the sloppy bastard kept all his contact details for the people he supplied, those he was blackmailing, and who supplied him. She knew about the rent officer, the 2 bank managers, which had sent her reeling when she realised they were in his business, and 2 high court judges.

God, how can they be let anywhere near a courtroom? she thought.

She also knew about high ranking police officers, teachers, and social workers who were involved with him.

Oh, God, I could get them all. Yes that's what I'll do. I'll make a plan, divorce him, make a new life, and maybe move to Spain. Oh joy! Yes, that's it, I'll teach the bastard a lesson he will never forget, and I'll get him locked up, she thought smiling to herself.

Suddenly, however, she realised to do all that, she would need some help. Who could she ask for help, because of course, everything she would tell them would have to be off the record? She instantly decided that the only one she could trust to stitch that bugger up like a kipper would be Claire Cummings.

She had 6 months to plan it.

"Take your time and act the subservient wife," she said out loud as if she had an audience in the car. "Yes I will thank you," she replied to herself.

She giggled out loud as she was driving to Colchester, and that's exactly what she decided to do.

Chapter 34

New ending

Well as they say, I suppose at the end, everything came out in the wash.

Once again the bonfire and gathering was a great success, and the whole street agreed that it was the best ever, and they were all looking forward to doing it all over again the following year. The saved chair that nearly drove Megan to distraction, actually rescued the family from eviction, and lots of prayers of thanks were said that night!

Megan finally passed her first cooking exam, even though it was almost sabotaged, and a brand new fund was set up in her school for disadvantaged children, so they would never have to worry about buying ingredients or supplies for any exam ever again.

The only person in her house who said 'well done' when the little postcard from the South West Exam Board landed on the carpet unexpectedly 3 months after the exam was over was Trixie. Megan smiled when she saw the A grade, and for the first time in years, she suddenly felt like she had accomplished something real and meaningful. It made it all better, and gave her the strength and resilience to carry on, even though it seemed others didn't want her to.

As for Sally - well it was raspberry pop and blackcurrant ice cream all round, when she called to congratulate Megan.

"Well done, Meg's I knew you could do it," she quietly whispered, and Patsy said nothing at all and just glared at the happy gathering in the kitchen as Sally dished out the pop and ice cream.

The rogue demon was put away, never to return and harm any living human or animal ever again, and despite Stuart dying, which was so sad, the biggest grief of all was the loss of his family, which to this day has never been explained.

Sally realised that she could not live without the children in her life, such was the impact they had had on her. She had also recovered well from her horrible ordeal with Harold. She vowed never to leave Megan and her siblings ever again, and was now living very happily in her new house just a 5 minute drive away.

Sergeant William Brown had his wrists slapped very hard by Claire Branning, and would remain under secret investigation for some time. His wife Louise went to live with her mother in Colchester to escape his wrath and embarrassment until the matter died down. He would deal with her later.

And as for Patsy? Never in all the history of the council painting department, had a house been painted and completed so quickly. The six man team, had both doors and front garden gate, and all the window frames, scraped, stripped and primer applied within hours. Beautiful bright yellow golden buttercup gloss was then painted liberally, once the primer had dried in the warm summer sunshine. The children screamed with delight as they ran up the road coming home from school that day and saw the freshly painted white window frames and the brightly painted yellow door and sparkling garden gate. Both had a large 'WET PAINT' sign hanging to the side of them.

It all ended fairly though. Patsy got her bright yellow doors and gate, despite Fred not wanting her to, and he got his well-deserved bonus cheque, and a very large one it was too, so much so, that he spent 2 weeks in Alicante with his wife soaking up the sun and Sangria.

And as for the rest of the street, the lovely dark red and blue and occasional green newly painted doors and gates looked very smart indeed!

Only one door stood out as a nicer colour than all the rest – the Murphy house, the little one with the bright yellow door!

And what of the demon I hear you ask? Well! He's still sat on the roof, waiting…

Epilogue

Demons

Explaining demons ref Stuart Green

What is a demon? I am often asked. I suppose the easiest way to talk about and explain them is this: they are a type of malevolent or evil spirit. They are derived from the Devil himself, and some say they are his henchmen. They are complete loners, have absolutely no worshippers or followers, and are really bad, bad boys and girls (they can be either).

They can travel from one world to another with complete ease, although it will always be in darkness as they hate the light. They move around in a very dark world looking for people who have the gift (psychics, sensitives and mediums usually) but also for those who are weak, as don't forget, we all have the gift, it's just some choose to either ignore it, or are not able to tune into this fascinating world.

Most people would never see, hear or sense them, and that's fine, it's not them they want, they want soft, sensitive, open people, so they can plant a seed around them to establish contact, frighten them, and pull them in. Demons feed on fear. They appear to everyone in a totally different form, depending on your personal fears. Once they have established contact, they start little by little, day by day, to talk to you, usually in your head, feeding you information, sucking out the essence of your soul, and daring you to take risks. They will change your personality, slowly feeding on your soul, drawing life away from you until you succumb to death, which will always be slow and painful, and very unpleasant.

On the other hand demons hate light: sunshine, laughter, singing, prayers, general happiness, and especially the Bible and the crucifix, but trust me if they set their sights on you, they won't give up easily.

The main thing is this! Never, never, never invite them to connect with you, and never invite them in. If you don't you are safe. Laugh, sing, be happy; they can't hurt you, but the minute you weaken and let them in, that's it, and unless you find a brilliant priest well practiced in exorcism, it's game over.

Lightning Source UK Ltd.
Milton Keynes UK
UKOW04f0807051017
310457UK00001B/220/P